FAE'S LOVE
FATED MATES OF THE FAE ROYALS, SUMMER COURT BOOK 8
HELEN WALTON

Walton House Publishing

WALTON HOUSE PUBLISHING

CONTENTS

FOREWARD

A UTHOR NOTE
Choosing character names is not always easy, and there are times you pick them to mean something for the character and the story. I've included the pronunciation and meaning of the names, and if you're like me, and like to know and still pronounce the names the way you read them, then welcome to my club.

Niamh pronounced neeve meaning radiance.

Fintan pronounced fin-tan meaning white fire.

Eamon pronounced aim-on meaning keeper of riches.

Maeve pronounced may-veh meaning intoxicating.

Diarmuid pronounced deer-mid meaning without enemy.

Orlaith pronounced or-lah meaning golden princess.

Rian pronounced ree-an means little king.

Briana pronounced bree-a-nah meaning noble.

Aislinn pronounced ash-lin meaning a vision or dream.

Saoirse pronounced seer-sha meaning freedom.

Lorcan pronounced lor-can meaning silent or fierce.

Ciara pronounced kee-ra meaning dark.

Roisin pronounced row-sheen meaning little rose.

Donagh pronounced done-acka meaning brown-haired warrior.

Deirdre pronounced deer-dree meaning broken-hearted.

Malachi pronounced mal-lah-key means messenger of God.

Fallon pronounced fa-len meaning descended from a ruler.

Ailbhe pronounced all-bay meaning white.

Tadhg pronounced tie-guh meaning poet or philosopher.

Eabha pronounced ey-ya meaning life.

Brandon pronounced bran-den meaning prince.

For the delicate rose is surrounded
by the love of thorns.

CHAPTER ONE
ROISIN

MY LEGS WERE NUMB from sitting in the chair for so long. The Summer Court palace was my home, my sanctuary, but right now I didn't want to be here. The urge to do something, anything, filled every inch of my being. Father, the Fae King, was dying. Mother wouldn't leave his side. I didn't blame her. Fated mates were everything to the Fae and my parents' love for each other was epic. The love of fairytales in the books inside our magical library. The stories my older sister, Ciara, read to me when I was younger and I didn't understand how to read a word. She and my other older brothers and sisters still considered me young even though I was the same age as Mother when she met Father.

I eased out of the chair and tiptoed from the room. Mother's focus stayed on Father's prone form. One last glance back at my dying father was all it took to send me out of the room. Blood rushed back to my numb legs. Pins and needles prickled my toes, but with each step along the marble hallways of the palace, the sensation lessened. By the time I reached the atrium where our Spring of Life flowed, the familiar, smooth cobblestones beneath my feet were the only sensation left to focus on.

Water gurgled slowly from the spring into the small stream beneath. The magical power in the palace's heart still seeped from every inch, even though the once spectacular atrium was now decaying from its former splendor. Over the last few years, the effects on the spring were so obvious, it was lucky only the Fae royals saw it for themselves.

I risked a glance over my shoulder to make sure no one noticed me in the atrium. No footsteps came padding down the hallway. No one was searching for me. They'd all assume I'd stay here in the Summer Court.

Sneaking out of the palace seemed easy. Too easy considering the lengths Father had gone to throughout hundreds of years to keep us safe after the tragic attack by the Trappers. I'd also grown up with those stories. The horrors we'd faced. Our almost extinction at the hands of evil humans. An icy chill ran down my spine. If they'd succeeded, I wouldn't be here today, and I was thankful for every day I had lived this beautiful life, but now our Spring of Life and the source of our immortality were dying like my father.

Perhaps one day we'd die too and all of Father's protections would have been for nothing, anyway.

Such a pessimistic outlook when I wasn't that way. My fingers rubbed against the sudden chill in my hands. My powers over ice made my hands glow like a snow-white crystal as I waved them in the air and called on the power of the Veil separating the Summer Court and Earth. The Veil swirled into view, a glistening curtain of magic the same color as my hands. I stepped into the curtain, sensing the magical vibrations on my skin. The power pulsed against my flesh as though it wanted free. Focusing on my sister, Aislinn, I stepped into an overrun garden. Aislinn's voice echoed from a short distance away but I didn't see her through the vines and rambling roses surrounding me. Relief shot through my veins as I successfully traveled through the Veil.

"Little sister, what are you doing here?" Lorcan, my beloved rascal of a brother, asked from behind me.

Startled, my power over the Veil dropped. Swirls of my white magic slithered back to my hands and up my arms. Ice covered them, but then it vanished, as did the magical portal in the blink of an eye. I'd started a new journey in my life.

"I'm not so little." My hands landed on my hips as I huffed out a breath.

"No, I suppose not." His eyes twinkled mischievously under the moonlit sky.

"Why must you antagonize your sisters?" Pepper, his fated mate and a witch no less, asked.

"Because it's fun." He shrugged.

I laughed, then hurried through the overgrown plants surrounding me to hug him. He ruffled the top of my hair as he hugged me back. My power flared in my hands and ice coated my palms, slithering up his back.

"Shite, Roisin." He pretended to shudder and stepped back. "Don't freeze me."

"That'll teach you to tease me." I tucked my hands behind my back, willing my power to ease so I wouldn't freeze everything around me.

"How is Father?" he asked.

I shook my head and turned my face as a lone tear trickled down my cheek, turning to a droplet of ice as it did so. Lucky for me, Fae didn't suffer from the cold, but now I was here on Earth, I'd have to temper my powers even more.

"Come on." Lorcan flung an arm over my shoulder. "We need all the help we can get."

Pepper gave me a wink and slid against the other side of Lorcan. He flung his other arm around her waist and kissed the top of her head. I never believed I'd see the day Lorcan would be so in love, but he, too, had found his fated mate.

When would it be my turn?

That should be the least of my worries, but it was the notion of fated love that kept all Fae strong throughout the many years.

Lorcan led us down a set of steps and into an underground building. People walked back and forth between a long table running down the center of the room and aisles upon aisles of bookshelves. Ciara and her best friend Malachi sat at the table, their heads bent over a book together. She must be in her element with so many books to read.

An old man with gray hair stepped forward, worry lines etched on his weathered skin.

"I'm Alister O'Cuinn, and who might you be?"

"This is my sister, Roisin," Lorcan said.

"We have more Fae here!" He grinned. "If this wasn't under such dire circumstances, then it'd call for a celebration."

He sounded like Mother and Father with their balls. A young man walked toward our small huddle. His stride was long and determined. Muscular legs like those of our King's guards tapered up to his tight waist. His broad chest expanded as he drew in a deep breath. My gaze snapped to his face. His striking blue eyes held me captive. I couldn't look away even as he stopped next to Alister.

"Grandfather, do you need help?"

"Brandon." Alister slapped him on his muscular shoulder. "Meet Fae Princess Roisin."

"Pleasure, I'm sure." He grinned, not once blinking or looking away from my face.

His gaze seemed to drink me in the same way I was with him. I couldn't explain the sudden obsession with a human. This wouldn't do. I lifted my chin in the air and broke our staring match.

There was no way I'd fall for the strikingly handsome human.

CHAPTER TWO
ROISIN

THE DAYS ON EARTH blended together. We'd spent hours upon hours every day researching the books in the Fellowship library. In those days, I'd spent every single one avoiding talking to Brandon. It didn't stop me from staring at him, though.

Or studying the magical bookshelf at the end of the library that they allowed no one to touch.

I'd somehow wound up standing in front of it yet again, even though my family had warned me not to touch any of the books on the shelves because they'd disappear if a person removed one book. It was a strange phenomenon to have a bookshelf in a library we couldn't touch. What was so special about the books? Or was it the shelf? I scanned the titles of each book yet again. The books appeared the same as all the other books in the library. Some titles were more obscure, while others were exact, and pretty designs etched others. All were leather-bound volumes. Sturdy in appearance.

"Roisin!"

I jolted back from the shelf.

"What were you doing?" Lorcan asked.

"Looking at the books."

"Make sure that's all you do," he said. "Come on, Ciara is about to try to fix the spring."

Turning our backs on the shelf, we strode from the library, up the stairs, and into the garden outside where the entire Fellowship stood waiting. Luckily, they hadn't seen me near the magical bookshelf.

After so long of searching, my sister Ciara had finally found a cure and now she was heading back to the Summer Court to fix our dying spring.

She lifted her hands and called on her powers. Magic swirled as the Veil opened to the Summer Court. It was a sight I'd only witnessed when watching my brothers and other sisters escape through the lock the Fae King, our father, had put on it many years ago. I'd never watched Ciara wield the Veil with her dark shadow magic. Like me, she'd only recently traveled to Earth. Everything had changed of late. Father had relinquished a fraction of his control and had opened a doorway through the Veil, but our dying Spring of Life meant our powers weren't performing how they should.

Ciara stepped into the swirling magic of the Veil, her shadow powers shot out, and grasped the hand of Sir Axis, the Water Sprite Master, in a last-bid attempt to fix our magical water. If he wasn't powerful enough to perform the task, as a being of immense waterpower, then we'd lose our immortality and die. A concept that had never occurred to any of us. I squinted my eyes as Sir Axis disappeared into the shadows and, in a way, became a part of Ciara.

Her best friend and recently discovered fated mate, Malachi, who'd swapped images with Sir Axis to trick the magic of the Veil, appeared distraught as the Veil closed and Ciara disappeared entirely from our sight. My brother Lorcan's fated mate, Pepper, a witch, had performed a spell on Malachi and Sir Axis to swap appearances. It was better than the alternative of Ciara marking Sir Axis as her mate, so he'd be able to travel through the Veil to the Summer Court because only Fae could travel there. All so the Water Sprite Master would fix our spring.

I had every faith in Ciara that she would be the one to find a cure for our problems. I hadn't expected it to bring her problems. We'd all been blind to the fact Malachi and Ciara were fated mates. No, that wasn't right. The declining spring had warped everything, and the locked Veil had altered everything, too.

Earth was the most damaged by our absence, according to everyone. Part of me sensed the disturbance in the realm, as though it was calling to my powers. The fabric of the realm was crying out in pain for me to heal it, but my powers over ice would more likely damage it than heal the realm. I wasn't sure what my part in this journey was, but I was here on Earth trying to find a future, my future.

My fate.

We all had one.

Saoirse was fated to find her wolf shifter mate, Arrow, near a magical waterfall. Briana was fated to find Sledge, a wolf shifter mate too, in the same location of Crystal Creek, so she helped Saoirse give birth to the newest Fae royal, Ailbhe. Rian was fated to save his jaguar shifter mate, Sophia, and move to Earth to be by her side as she ruled the Amazon Jungle. Lorcan was fated to find Pepper, a witch who had led us back to Saltine, our long-ago witch seer who'd helped us vanquish the Trappers. Aislinn was fated to find her long-lost fated mate Fallon on Earth, which led to the discovery of this place and the Fellowship of the Infinite Spring, which was connected to our Spring of Life. Ciara was fated to Malachi all along, but their journey to a secret magical location above the waterfall led them to the Water Sprites who were about to help cure our spring.

Was there anything left for me to do?

I pressed a finger between my eyes.

"Are you all right?" Aislinn asked.

Ever since she'd found her fated mate, she'd become less inclined to lead with her daggers, and more open to discussing feelings. It was a tad strange to see her transformation, but I suppose love did that to people.

I dropped my hand. "I'm fine."

"Oh, aye, we're all fine." Her fingers stroked the hilt of the dagger strapped to her waist.

"We will be," I said, standing up tall and forcing a smile onto my face. "Ciara will do this."

Aislinn's gaze softened. "You always have so much faith in all of us."

"Of course, you're my family. If I can't believe in you, then who can I believe in?"

A slight pink tinged her cheeks.

"I have a lot of apologizing to do," she said.

"For what?"

"I was so angry and unhappy for so long. I'm ashamed to admit I took it out on you and the others." Her blush deepened.

"You weren't so bad." I shrugged.

Aislinn laughed meekly, then surprised me with a hug. I squeezed her back and let out a sigh.

"You can tell me anything," she whispered into my ear.

"Aye," I whispered back, then released her, clearing my throat of the emotions between us. "I honestly don't know. It's like this weight or pressure on me. I'm supposed to be doing something important."

Aislinn's brows dipped into a frown. "Were you meant to go back with Ciara?"

I shook my head. "No. It's this place." I pointed to the stairs leading to the underground library.

"We have a lot more to research in those books. Perhaps that's it?"

"Maybe." I sighed.

Aislinn gasped. A strange sensation ran through my body and tingled every inch of my skin. She grabbed my arm.

"Did you sense that?"

"Aye."

"She did it." She released my arm and placed her hands over her mouth.

"Of course, Ciara found the cure." I resisted the urge to roll my eyes. None of my brothers and sisters believed my faith in Ciara, but I'd known all along she'd succeed.

Aislinn shook her arms. "I haven't experienced this much power for years."

I lifted my hands and grimaced at the ice lining the tips of my fingers. My power had surged with the cure of the spring, but thankfully, I hadn't iced the entire secret garden even if the garden was decrepit and overgrown. Imagine if I'd frozen everyone here. All the Fellowship members who'd tried to help us. My gaze slid to one member in particular.

Brandon O'Cuinn.

Dark and dangerous in looks. He wore a black jacket with a black T-shirt. I'd learned the names of everyone since coming here, but it was Brandon who was stuck in my mind. His pants were black too and highlighted the tight muscles of his legs and the firm roundness... Heat filled my face and I glanced at the ground, willing my racing hormones to calm. The way I felt around him was inexplicable and who would I ask about the strange emotions I was experiencing? Every time I looked at him, my heart raced. No other man had attracted me. Not until Brandon. My family hadn't been around humans for centuries, and while I'd heard the stories of Fae finding love with humans, we all knew we'd never be able to mark them as our mates. Human bodies weren't strong enough for our powers. While we might be compatible in some ways, we'd never be fated to each other. This was my first time around humans. I fingered the folds of my rainbow-colored dress. I hadn't changed into human clothing yet. Well, I had for a day while one of the Fellowship members cleaned my dress, but I'd quickly returned to wearing my familiar dress as soon as possible.

A heated gaze on my face made me drag my attention from the unruly plants around my feet to find Brandon's dark blue gaze studying me. I'd caught him looking at me many times. He'd tried talking to me many times too, but I'd fled in the other direction. Words tangled on my tongue in his presence. There was no point admitting Brandon appealed to me. Fae couldn't mark a human as their mate. I'd kill him. He didn't deserve to die because I found him attractive. His gaze snared mine for a moment before I followed the contours of his face to the dark stubble lining his cheeks and chin. The darkness surrounded the pale pink of his lips. My gaze stayed on them for a moment too, before the heat returned to my face. I longed to escape his proximity.

Brandon's grandfather, the leader of the Fellowship, stepped beside him and his intense gaze left me. The loss was instantaneous, as though every cell in my body craved his attention.

I glanced around the group, who were all celebrating. Now was my chance to do the one thing I'd wanted since I saw it inside the library.

CHAPTER THREE
BRANDON

I'D TRAINED FOR YEARS to join the Fellowship of the Infinite Spring, but those studies had not prepared me for meeting real Fae and witches who performed spells that changed people's appearances. The stunning beauty of the Fae princess Roisin stunned me the most. No matter the stories I'd heard from Grandfather or the books he'd read me in my childhood, and the way he'd instilled I'd be the next leader of the Fellowship after him. None of those things seemed to stay in my mind whenever I looked at Roisin.

Every time I looked at her, my heart missed a beat. It was like the sight of her made every cell in my body alive, but she'd barely acknowledged I existed in the short time we'd been studying in the library together. Every time I came close to her, she walked the other way. I'd seen her talking to Grandfather and other Fellowship members, but she avoided me at all costs. It was strange and intriguing.

The air shimmered with magic inside the walls of the enclosed garden around the Infinite Spring. To be human and experience magic was something else. Yet these beings had access to it every second of the day. They were strong while we were weak and at their mercy. I hated every second feeling at their mercy.

I wanted to be the one to cure Earth. Humans lived on Earth, and even though I'd read about the Fae once living in harmony here with us, my mind struggled with the concept of magic in our everyday lives. These powerful creatures who could annihilate us and then the entire planet, if they wanted, had been our friends and lovers.

My gaze skidded to Roisin. What would it be like to love a woman so powerful? To have her love me back?

She brushed her hands up and down her thighs over the long rainbow skirt of her dress as though trying to warm them or ease an ache which, from what I understood about Fae, was unlikely as they didn't experience either.

"Well," Lorcan said. "I guess all we can do is wait now."

"Aye," Roisin mumbled through her pretty pink lips.

Shit, now I was thinking about her lips. I needed to get out of here and get laid or something. It'd been months since I'd enjoyed being with a woman. With all the training and studying, I hadn't the time to even contemplate sex, but looking at Roisin, sex was all I thought about.

Malachi smiled at me as though he'd read my thoughts. As though he, too, understood my lustful thoughts for Fae princesses. I shifted uncomfortably under his scrutiny. His form now looked like Sir Axis and the Water Sprite Master was a bizarre creature. Arrogant and conceited with an air of authority that rubbed my grandfather, Alister, the wrong way every time he spoke. Grandfather had said he couldn't wait for him to leave, but I worried about a powerful being who had the magic to influence water and what that would mean for Earth. Imagine if he stopped all our water flowing. We'd die in no time at all.

Suddenly, the atmosphere shifted. Power vibrated through the air, up from the soil, and in every molecule around us. How I recognized the magic, I wasn't sure, but Malachi's body once again became his.

"She did it," Roisin said. A huge smile spread her lips and made her cheeks rosy with her happiness.

"Aye," Lorcan said, a smile lighting his face too.

"Take me to her," Malachi said.

Perhaps there was more between Princess Ciara and Malachi than I'd first guessed. It wouldn't be the first time I'd missed signs of the romantic nature. I didn't believe in love after the way Father had vanished. Mother said he'd left a note saying he couldn't handle his life. Grandfather wouldn't talk about him. We were all angry he'd left without a trace and forsaken his family. If I was romantic, I'd imagine he'd died protecting Mother, but he'd left because this life was too hard. Signing over every part of ourselves to the Fellowship wasn't for everyone. The thing that hurt the most was knowing I was part of the reason he'd left. I was part of his life. A baby at the time. What couldn't he handle about a baby? The fact he had a son? What sort of man leaves his child?

After finishing the training, I understood the strains of life living in the Fellowship too well. There had been times I'd considered quitting, but there were more times I'd sensed deep inside me I was on the right path and heading to a destination that was meant for me and me alone.

Whatever that destination was.

Lorcan, Pepper, and Malachi disappeared through the shimmering magic of the Veil. Aislinn and Fallon embraced in a hug.

And Roisin...

She snuck down the stairs that led to the underground library of the Fellowship.

I wasted a minute waiting for Grandfather to leave my side before sneaking down the stairs after her.

CHAPTER FOUR
ROISIN

THE AIR WAS A tad musty in the underground library. Not as fresh as the air outside in the garden. Golden lights lit the staircase as I padded down the stone steps and hurried across the floor, passing rows upon rows of bookshelves. The long table in the center of the room was a warm, well-worn timber that once would have been a magnificent tree. I trailed my fingers along the edge. Had our Fae ancestors helped the Fellowship build this library? It seemed plausible to me if the stories about us living in harmony were true.

And they were. Father and Mother had told me the stories themselves. They would never lie to me or my brothers and sisters. We were family, even though our royal duty was to the Summer Court and our Spring of Life.

My power had never been more at ease since Ciara fixed the spring. There was no longer the constant pressure of ice wanting to escape from my hands. I could let out a sigh of relief. I glanced around and did just that. The sound echoed inside the enormous library. I covered my mouth to stop from giggling, so no one heard it echo too.

I had little time before everyone noticed my absence. Even though I didn't have Fae royal guards with me, my brother and sister were too observant and too protective. They'd notice I was missing and follow me, but I wouldn't let them stop me. Nor would I let the Fellowship members stop me from testing my theory.

The Fellowship was all about following rules to keep order and protect the Infinite Spring that ran from a fountain wall inside this secret place. We comprehended little about the Fellowship. We'd only recently learned of their existence. Which was the strangest thing I'd ever heard. A secret society to protect the Fae that the Fae didn't know existed.

There were so many questions yet to be answered.

Ciara might have saved us from mortality, but there was more to be discovered. I was certain of it.

My feet stopped moving as I reached my destination.

I'd reached the bookshelf at the end of the library, but this was no ordinary bookshelf. This was a magical one where if humans took a book from the shelf, the entire collection of books would disappear and a new collection would replace them. The Fellowship said they'd lost many important books on the shelf and didn't take a book from the shelves any longer because of it.

I saw it as an opportunity to learn more.

Who'd placed the magic on the shelves? Was it a Fae? Witch? Or other? And why? Why would a magical bookshelf take books away and not give them back? Was someone playing a game with these humans? Or giving them clues?

My family didn't consider I was the smartest. They saw me as the artist, the one who painted pretty pictures and wrote beautiful poems. There was more to me than the creative side. I had a fully functioning mind that was good for other things. That's why I was here. There was a book on the shelf that had an obscure image on the spine, but I believed it had a hidden meaning.

The Fellowship wouldn't let me take the book. My family needed their help, so they would never have listened to me if I'd said we needed that book. They were all blind to what was right in front of our faces.

There was nothing special in appearance about this bookshelf. Someone had made it from the same wood as the other shelves in the library. Displayed in a neat and ordered fashion sat the spines of the books. The bright lights in the library glinted off the titles. There were so many to choose from that if I'd loved books as much as Ciara, then I'd bet my fingers would itch to take every single book from the shelves. But I had one goal.

One book to take.

So what if the others disappeared, and we'd never see them again? They had to go somewhere when they disappeared, so the books couldn't be lost forever. Simply lost to us. For now, at least, because if the book had the clues in it we needed, then we'd find all the knowledge that was lost to us. We'd find our history, the history of the Fellowship, and how we were all connected.

How our power would help heal this realm.

How we'd become what we once were, but even better with the knowledge we would now possess.

As it was, my fingers itched to paint the bookshelf and have a reminder of this place and moment in time. I'd already sketched it with paper and ink, but it was in black and white. There were no vibrant colors, and I loved color. The more color, the better. That was why I wore rainbow-colored dresses.

Every world deserves color. Happiness. Love.

I aimed to bring it to everyone.

My hand reached for the book with the navy-blue cover and the tiny words Sarod embedded on the spine, hidden amongst the other letters that only I'd noticed with my artistic nature. I'd hidden words in my paintings too sometimes that no one in my family had ever noticed. No wonder I was the only one who'd noticed this clue.

CHAPTER FIVE
BRANDON

MY HEART HAMMERED INSIDE my chest as I saw Princess Roisin reach for a book on the magical shelf. I ran toward her, my hands reaching out to stop her from taking a book and making the others disappear. I might not have been here long, but I'd learned of the bookshelf during my studies. Learned the Fellowship let no one take a book from the shelf, otherwise we'd lose even more knowledge.

"Wait!" My hands clasped her shoulders, but it was too late. Her fingers closed around the spine of the book, and she jolted under my touch as though I'd zapped her with enough electricity to make her gasp.

The force threw us forward, and the air shimmered around us with even more magic that kept pulling us forward.

"What the hell!"

Roisin staggered forward toward the bookshelf, taking me with her since I was still holding her in an iron-tight grip. I couldn't let her go even if I wanted to, but I didn't.

It was my duty to protect the Fae, even though there was an extra protective urge coming from me when I thought about Roisin.

"Let go," Roisin said, deepening her usually sweet voice and making me realize she wasn't all sugar and sweetness like I first thought.

The pulling sensation intensified and tugged Roisin off her feet, and me with her, into the bookcase. I braced for the solid collision, but the timber frame of the bookcase disappeared. We fell through the glittering white of magical air for what seemed like hours but must have been seconds.

Roisin landed on the ground, her arm stretched above her head, stopping the book from hitting the snow-covered ground. I slammed into her back and quickly rolled away from crushing the Fae princess.

"Sorry," I said, offering her my hand as I stood.

She pushed to her feet as though she hadn't just landed on a snow-covered field and had a solid man slam into her dainty back. I supposed the Fae were stronger than humans, and I needed to remember that whenever I thought about Roisin. Which was way too much. She'd been warm beneath my body, and I'd longed to lie there and have her curves press into my body for longer.

I cleared my throat and shoved away the thoughts of her perfect body pressed against me.

"Where are we?"

Roisin shrugged and then hugged the book to her chest. "I assumed it was a clue, but I didn't consider this would happen."

I frowned. "What was a clue?"

"The book." She lifted it from her tight embrace and showed me the cover.

There was nothing spectacular about the book. It had tiny gold swirls in the corners and a single title on the cover that didn't even say a word I recognized.

"Okay, Princess." I shivered and wrapped my arms around my chest. "I have no clue what you're talking about, so lay it out in plain English."

Her pretty pink lips tipped up into a smile. I smiled back at her, for how could I not? She was so pretty, it hurt my eyes to look at her.

"I had a suspicion the magical bookshelf was more than an exchange for books. More than someone controlling what the Fellowship read, but I didn't expect it to be a doorway." She pointed to the title of the book and the delicate lines inside the words that looked like designs, but as she traced her finger over them, other letters stood out. How hadn't I noticed the hidden word? "See, it says door," she said. "I should have thought about it better. My family might be right about me not being smart."

"Okay." I held up my hand. "One thing at a time here." I resisted the urge to clatter my teeth together in the freezing cold. "Most importantly, I've met your family, and I doubt they consider you dumb."

She laughed. "No, they'd never call me dumb, but they always treat me like I'm young and understand nothing at all."

"That's different."

"How so?" She hugged the book to her chest again.

I rubbed my hands up and down my biceps, glad I was wearing a coat, but it wasn't a thick enough coat to withstand the cold from the snow.

"I'm the youngest member of the Fellowship, so I understand how elders treat young people, even though I'm next in line to be their leader."

Roisin huffed. "I'm fifty years old."

"You beat me. I'm twenty-five," I said. "That's like a quarter of life in terms of a human life span. What about fifty for Fae?"

She scowled. "Fifty is insignificant compared to how long we live. Although we almost lost our immortality, so if that had happened, then it would have been half my life."

"I'm glad Ciara fixed the spring. I can't imagine you already living half your life."

Her scowl dropped, and pink lit her cheeks. She was even prettier when she blushed. Which she seemed to do when she was around me. This was the longest conversation we'd had, and I didn't want it to stop.

A cold shudder ran up my back. "Where are we?"

"I'm not sure." She lifted the book and opened it. "I can't read any of it."

"Why not?"

"There are no words in here." She turned the open book around and showed me the blank pages.

"Well, shit, what do we do now? It's not like there's a bookshelf to put the book back on."

I glanced around. Snowy fields stretched for miles upon miles. A snow-covered tree stood here and there, but nothing that would offer protection from the elements. In the distance, the sides of dark rocks jutted through the snowy fields. I squinted as sunlight glinted off the snow, giving the false hope it'd warm me, but I'd freeze to death soon if we didn't find a warm place.

"No." Roisin frowned, but then her gaze fell on the sunbeams streaming through the cold air. "This place would be so lovely to paint."

"How about if we find a warm place, you paint it, then?"

Her gaze turned from the beauty of the sight, then her frown returned as she noticed me shivering.

"You're cold."

"Yeah." I cupped my hands and blew warm air into them.

The tip of my nose was already turning to ice. I wasn't a vain person, but I didn't want to lose my nose or my fingers and toes to frostbite.

"We should leave... but how?"

Power flared into her hands. "I can't travel through the Veil."

"No magic?"

"I have power, but with the lock still in place, it's difficult to access here."

"Never mind. I can't travel through your Veil, anyway."

"If I was like my brothers, I would command my power and make you a fire." Her chin dipped as she stared at the ground, the glowing in her palms fading into nothing. "I'm sorry."

"It's not your fault."

She lifted the book. "I took a book without permission, and you were trying to stop me, so aye, this is my fault."

"When you put it like that...."

Her gaze snapped to mine, and I laughed.

"You find this funny?"

"It's better to laugh and get on with things than cry over our mistakes."

"Aye," she said, straightening her shoulders. "We should find you shelter."

"Agreed. Which way?"

"They all look the same. I guess we take our chances?"

"Let's go." I started walking and already my feet were like blocks of ice to walk on.

Perhaps I would lose toes after all. The expanse of snow stretched before us in a never-ending field of icy nothingness. If we didn't find shelter, I'd lose my life.

CHAPTER SIX
ROISIN

T HE LONGER WE WALKED, the bluer Brandon's skin turned.

"Tell me what it's like being human."

If I distracted him from the cold, then I might ease his suffering.

His shoulders lifted in a half-hearted shrug as though he didn't have the energy to lift them further.

"I'm different from other humans. They don't know about Fae, whereas I do." His breath puffed as he spoke, sending clouds of icy air from his face. "I grew up knowing we were special. The chosen ones to protect you."

"Are the Fellowship good people?"

"The best." His icy eyelashes blinked heavily. "Grandfather is the best of them. One day I will be too."

"I'm sure you will be." I smiled grimly.

He chuffed out a laugh. "You don't sound so certain, Princess."

"I know nothing about humans nor the Fellowship."

"What would you like to know?"

"Anything. Everything."

His blue lips cracked as he smiled.

"Grandfather is the leader of the Fellowship. Ever since I could read, he's been training me to take over as the next leader."

"Should there have been someone between you two? He seems ancient, yet you're young."

His chin dropped to his chest. "My father, but he left when I was a baby."

"I'm sorry."

"Don't be. He left a note saying he couldn't handle the responsibility."

"Brandon." I gasped and placed a hand on his arm. "That's terrible."

His gaze slid to my hand, and I dropped it quickly.

"I know. That's why I don't spend any time thinking about him. He doesn't think about me."

"I truly am sorry." I stepped closer to him. "My father has always been there for me, for all of us. He may have done some questionable things to keep us safe, but we know he loves us. I'm sorry you don't know what it's like to have a father's love."

"Alister stepped in and loved me more than a grandson, but... I don't think it was the same."

"He sounds like a good man."

"He's the best." His lips cracked even more, drops of blood welled on the surface of his blue skin, then froze in place.

Perhaps I shouldn't have talked to him.

I was thankful I didn't suffer from the cold as humans did, but a weird pang tugged inside my chest at the notion I might have made a huge mistake and would cause Brandon's death.

It wasn't like I realized the book would take us to this other realm. I was certain we were no longer on Earth because the sun hadn't moved and in the short time I'd been on Earth, I'd witnessed the rise and fall of the sun. Our footfalls crunched on the snow, the only sound to be heard in this eerie environment since we'd stopped talking.

From what I understood about the realms, we were most likely in the Winter Court, but I couldn't confirm or deny it without proof. Proof meant meeting the demons that lived here. I'd heard they were hideous creatures with horns, wings, fangs, or talons, depending on the type of demon. I didn't want to alarm Brandon, either. Humans thought demons were evil. Demons were simply another supernatural creature.

Fae hadn't seen demons since Father had sealed the Veil separating our world from Earth. I remembered Ciara showing me one book she'd found on the Winter Court and how we'd talked about visiting the other courts one day. Imagine if she understood I was here. She'd ask me so many questions right now, like Brandon had as we'd started walking, but he'd fallen silent now.

"Brandon."

"Yeah?"

"What can I do to help you?"

His dark blue gaze landed on my face. "Find a way back. Tell my grandfather I died doing my job."

"You will not die. I won't let you." I grabbed his biceps in my hands. They were firm and muscular beneath my tight grip. "Didn't you learn anything about surviving in the snow?"

"I usually go out in snow gear and have a way to communicate with people. I've never been stuck in the snow."

Panic swirled low in my stomach. I'd dragged Brandon into this mess. I needed to get him out of it, but we'd seen nothing in the long time we'd walked. Nothing and no one that would help us. I cursed my impetuous nature for taking the book. Of thinking I'd find more answers. There had to be something I could do. My powers were over ice, and that would only make him colder. What if I froze him solid? I could preserve him.

My sister Saoirse had told me of the time Father froze her fated mate in a block of ice, but Saoirse's fated mate was a wolf shifter and not human. Would a human survive freezing?

"I don't know what to do." I dug my fingers into his arms, wishing for something to come to me.

"Relax. Breathe. I'm not dying right this second."

I huffed out a breath of warm air that gusted over his face with us being so close. His blue lips tugged up into a smile.

"If I was about to die, would you grant me a dying wish?"

"Anything."

"How about a kiss from a Fae princess?" His left eyebrow rose in challenge.

I released his arms and laughed. "You wouldn't want a kiss from the ice princess if you're freezing to death."

"One, you're not an ice princess, and two, the cold wouldn't matter right now." Another shiver ran over his body.

He'd started shivering less often now. I wasn't sure what that meant, but I didn't like the look of it.

"My powers are over ice, so aye, I'm an ice princess."

"Perhaps." He tilted his head to the side. "Ice princess means different on Earth."

"What does it mean?"

"A beautiful woman that is insanely hard to get because they interact with almost no one."

I wrapped my arms over my chest. "I'd say the Fae who call me that in the Summer Court mean the same thing."

"They're wrong and I'll take great pleasure in telling them so myself."

I snorted a laugh, then covered my mouth with a hand.

"From what I've seen of you, you're stunningly beautiful and have a sparkling personality that uplifts others. There is nothing icy about you."

I called my power to my hands and let the ice coat them. "And yet, here I am, ice and all."

"I don't believe it, and to prove it, you'll promise to kiss me before I die."

I couldn't help but smile at his arrogance. At his certainty that I would make such a promise. I could be as arrogant as him, though.

A smile tugged at the corners of my lips. "I'll promise you a dying kiss only because you won't die here."

He chuckled. "Princess, I'm not Fae like you. This cold will kill me, eventually."

I swallowed the lump of fear he was right. A part of me desired to know what it'd be like to kiss Brandon. If he was dying anyway, then I'd never fall for him. Never long to put my mark on his chest when I knew it would kill him. I stepped closer.

A swooshing noise sounded in the sky. We both looked up, shielding our eyes from the bright sunlight as a dark shadow passed over our heads. Within the time it took to blink, the unusual form landed in front of us.

A tall woman, taller than any I'd ever encountered, with horns on top of her head and a set of leathery wings behind her back, stared at us as though we were specimens in a jar.

"What little ants do I have here?" she asked. "Who dares come to the Winter Court unannounced? The King will have your heads."

"Quicker than freezing to death," Brandon said.

Her gaze snapped at him, and she gasped. "A human."

Then her gaze snapped at me. "And you, who are you?"

"I'm Fae Princess Roisin O'Cleirigh."

The demon stepped back. "This changes everything."

"And who are you?" I asked, not letting her enormous form intimidate me.

"You can call me Tay. Demon Princess of the Winter Court."

Beside me, Brandon gasped, and then he collapsed on the ground.

"No." I rushed to his side. "He can't die. This is all my fault."

Tay tilted her horned head to the side. "How did you both get here?"

I lifted the book I still had clutched in my hand.

"How did you get that?" She reached for the book, but I snatched it back toward my body.

"I'll tell you as soon as you help my friend."

"Let's get one thing straight, princess to princess. I don't take kindly to blackmail."

"I'm not blackmailing you. I simply want to get my friend out of the cold before he dies before we talk. Please."

Tay's black demon eyes narrowed. "If you're fooling me, then your death won't be fast."

"I'm not fooling you. I wouldn't even know how. This is my first time leaving the Summer Court."

"Oh, yes, we know all about what your father has done."

I didn't like the way she said that, but she scooped Brandon up in her arms. Jealousy pounded hard in my veins that she was holding him so close to her body when it was me he'd made a promise to kiss him before he died. I shoved it aside because I shouldn't have those feelings for a human. I'd never be able to mark him as my mate because he'd die from the sheer power of it. A kiss before dying meant nothing, but jealousy meant emotions, feelings...

Tay launched into the air, taking Brandon with her.

"No," I screamed.

Had she tricked me?

CHAPTER SEVEN
BRANDON

I WOKE UP WITH a heavy weight on my body. Warmth filled every limb in a delicious haze that I thought I'd never experience again after almost dying in the snow. Wait. I sat up with a start and opened my eyes. An opulent bedroom filled with deep red furnishings met my startled gaze. The thick blankets covering my body slid to my waist relieving the heavy sensation.

A feminine gasp dragged my attention to the chair by the fireplace. Roisin sat in the ornate gothic chair, the flames from the fire licking over her skin in the way I'd imagined kissing her the second after I'd made her promise to kiss me before I died. I regretted I hadn't died because I'd missed out on that kiss.

"You're finally awake," Roisin said.

"How long have we been here?" I rasped out through a dry throat. It felt like I hadn't drunk water in days.

Roisin shrugged. "It's hard to tell when the sun doesn't set. They have months of light and then months of darkness. Tay said we were lucky we came in the light months because you would have frozen long before she found us if we'd arrived in the dark months."

I wriggled my fingers and toes expecting pain like I'd heard about from frostbite, but every inch of my body felt good. Spectacular actually, going by the twitch in my cock from thinking about asking Roisin to join me in bed so we'd celebrate my survival with more than a kiss. I choked on a laugh imagining how horrified her expression would be, especially with how hard it was to get her to promise me a kiss. Why was my first thought upon waking about Roisin?

"How do you feel?" she asked shifting in the chair and sending the light spilling over her chest. I swear I saw her nipples through the sheer material of the dress she was now wearing. It wasn't the rainbow-colored dress she normally wore. This one was white. Very bridal night.

And there went my cock to full hardness. I plucked one pillow from behind my head and placed it over my lap. Roisin's blue eyes with the indigo ring watched every movement I made. I'd like to imagine she was appreciating my bare chest, but she might be assessing me for harm.

"I feel surprisingly good for almost dying. At least I did my duty and kept you safe." I glanced around the room. The enormity of my almost death sinking in. What if I'd died while trying to protect Roisin? What if no one ever discovered where we were? Grandfather would be so disappointed in me if I'd died from extreme weather. He'd instilled in me from a young age my duty and responsibilities to the Fae. And here I was lusting after a Fae Princess of all women. Yet, there was a thudding in my head that said my feelings for her were more than just lust. If only I could find out if she felt anything for me. It might be wrong for me to feel this way, but I'd never been surer of anything in my life even after the short time we'd spent together. "You were safe while I was unconscious?"

"I was with you the entire time and perfectly safe."

"Who undressed me?"

A blush filled her face. "Tay insisted on having a servant do it. She said she'd heal you better that way."

I swiped my tongue over my dry lips. "The demon..." I couldn't believe I said that. "Healed me?"

"She did. You would have lost fingers and toes if she hadn't, so I agreed to it."

"Thank you." I wriggled my fingers trying to stop imagining losing them.

How would I have been a member of the Fellowship without fingers and toes? I wouldn't. They would have retired me before I'd even really begun my journey as a member of the Fellowship. Before I even became their leader.

I suppose I had to thank a demon.

"Demons are real?"

"Oh, aye."

"Huh, I should have expected that." I massaged the muscles on the back of my neck.

Roisin's gaze followed the line of my bicep down to my bare chest, and if I wasn't mistaken, I'd say that was a very appreciative feminine look. Thank God for the pillow over my cock because it jumped even more at the notion she liked the way I looked.

"Want to join me in bed?" I winked.

She jerked her head sideways and stared into the fireplace. A dark black mantel piece surrounded the glowing yellow-orange flames.

"You learned the stories of the Trappers?" she said changing the subject and not addressing the sexual tension between us. I'd let it go, but this pull between us was stronger every time I looked at her, which was a lot. She'd have to talk to me about it one day and I'd wait all my life if I had to. However long that was. I'd almost died guarding her in this new realm. Death might not scare her, but it did me now. I'd never thought about my death until I was on its doorstep. All the things I'd studied for, the training I'd endured so that one day I'd be the next leader of the Fellowship would have been for nothing. Keeping Roisin alive was my duty, yet there was more to my feelings for her than a responsibility. They scared me more than this realm. Excited me more than completing my training and entering the Fellowship as a full-fledged member.

"Yes." There went the raging hardness of my cock as my thoughts turned to the atrocities the Trappers inflicted on the Fae. All because we'd failed in our role as protectors of the Infinite Spring, and they'd drank from the magical water becoming tainted and power-hungry.

"It's strange seeing a fire. I've read about them, but words can't describe the heat caressing my skin from the golden glow of the dancing flames." She lifted her hand toward the fireplace. Ice crystals formed on her palm and then melted in an instant, dropping water to the timber floor at her feet.

"Fire and ice," I whispered.

"They don't mix well together, do they?"

"Total opposites," I agreed.

"I can't imagine what my family went through." She shuddered as though she'd imagined it. "I'm so different from my siblings. My parents. Even though Ciara was a babe in our mother's womb at the time, she too was still a part of it, whereas I wasn't."

"Hey." I flung back the sheet overwhelmed with the need to comfort her and forgetting my lack of clothing, but the warm air in the room hit my naked body. I yanked on the thick blanket and wrapped it around my waist, dragging it with me as I walked over to her. Kneeling before her, I took her hand. It was cold to my touch even though she was by the warmth of the fire. She stared into the flickering flames as though mesmerized by their display. "Look at me."

Her pretty gaze fell on my face. Surprise flitted through them, and she tried to tug her hand away, but I held on tight.

"There's nothing wrong with being different."

"Isn't there?"

"No."

"They all treat me differently."

I stroked a thumb over the back of her hand. Her skin was soft. Every second I held onto her, the delicate skin warmed, chasing away the cold of her ice powers.

"I don't have siblings."

"And?" she asked with a royal haughtiness that made my cock twitch again. I liked her sass.

"But I imagine if I had a younger sister, I'd be extra protective of her. I'm sure that's why they treat you differently. My dad left when I was young. I grew up being very protective of my ma. It was hard being away from her while studying for the Fellowship. I'd say your family is the same way with you."

"Aye, they've been trying to find a cure for the spring for years. I always recognized Ciara would be the one to fix it."

"But you didn't stick around to talk to her about it."

"Dia, no. They would never have let me take a book from the magical shelves. Let alone travel to another realm. You should have seen how appalled they were to find out I was at the Fellowship."

"We'd let no harm come to a Fae." I stroked my thumb over the back of her hand again. "I'd let no harm come to you."

A smile pulled her pretty lips up. "You almost froze to death. How would you have stopped me from being harmed?"

I choked on a laugh since she had a point.

A delicate giggle escaped her lips making me long to kiss her yet again. I leaned toward her, testing the pull between us. She didn't back down, but as I was on my knees in front of her, I was in a more submissive position. Perhaps that's why our attraction didn't threaten her. Didn't she realize this position gave me a direct line of sight to her breasts, which were indeed covered by white sheer fabric? Her pert nipples begged for my mouth to cover them and tease them into even harder peaks.

Shit. I had it bad for the Fae Princess.

My gaze traveled lower to the junction of her legs, but she was firmly squeezing her thighs together as though she was keeping them glued shut on purpose. What would it take to get her to open them wide for me? My tongue darted along my teeth. What would she taste like? She smelled delicious, her scent growing more aromatic by the second next to the fire, or was it because of me being next to her? Me being so close I almost tasted her arousal.

"Brandon?" she whispered as though once again caught in a haze.

I sure was. A haze of lust and desire for Roisin and more going by the thud of my heart in my chest. I dragged my gaze back to her face. Her cheeks flushed a pale pink reminding me of the petals of a pink rosebud.

"Roisin? As delicate as a rose." I lifted my other hand and stroked her cheek with the backs of my fingers, unable to keep from touching her any longer. Sparks of electricity danced up my fingers to my arm and along the back of my scalp.

She gasped as though she'd experienced the connection between us. Roisin's eyes widened, then she jerked her head back and shoved me hard in the chest with ice-covered hands.

"Are you as prickly as a rose too? Will you scar me if I get close?" I exhaled. All I wanted was her, and I'd take her prickles, all the scars she'd give me if only she'd give us a chance. Maybe my almost death had made things clearer for me because I couldn't deny this magnetism she had over me. Being in this magical kingdom changed me because I felt stronger here.

Perhaps it was Roisin who'd changed me?

CHAPTER EIGHT
ROISIN

WHAT THE DIA WAS I doing? About to kiss a human. Fall for his charm and then what? Nothing. There couldn't be anything between us. I wouldn't love him. Couldn't mark him as my mate. It would kill him. My power refused to abate though as though it wanted to mark him as mine. I didn't understand why it would act that way when he was a human.

"What were you doing?" I stood and paced to the window covered in a thick black velvet curtain, I yanked the heavy material aside and gazed out at the snow-lit wonder of the realm.

"We were talking."

The blankets made a rustling noise as Brandon must have stood.

"Talking?" I spun around.

"Yes, it's what people do."

"Don't get smart with me." I placed my hands on my hips.

"What do you want me to say?" His hands slackened around the blanket, and it slipped even further down his waist revealing the intriguing trail of hair on his lower stomach and the sharp lines of the muscles beside his hips. "That I'm wildly attracted to you? That I can't stop thinking about kissing you? Touching every inch of your body until you're exhausted from orgasm after orgasm."

My mouth fell open. Never had a man said anything like that to me. Heated arousal pooled between my legs. My body responded to his words. To the hard swell of his cock beneath the blankets. I'd longed to spread my legs before him while sitting on the chair to see what he'd do with the invitation. I guess I knew now he'd take anything I offered him, but would it be fair to use him for his body? For the orgasms he said he'd give me.

"But..."

"But what?" He quirked an eyebrow.

"But Fae have fated mates."

His gaze fell to the floor for a second, then he raised his chin. "From what I've read, you might wait hundreds of years for your fated mate. Don't you want to live in the moment? You almost lost your immortality. Would you have kept waiting for him then?"

"That is a moot point. I always believed we'd fix the spring."

"Okay, Princess Roisin, wait for your fated one." He spun around and strode across the room toward the door leading to the bathing chambers. "Can you find my clothes while I wash up? Then my naked chest won't tempt you to stare at it like you have been since I woke."

With that, he flung open the door and shut it with a finality that left me aching to have his presence back.

I turned back to the window and pressed my forehead against the cool glass pane. There was a call to the snow-covered realm outside that made me feel like I belonged there. It was such a strange sensation since I'd grown up in the warmth of the Summer Court. I couldn't explain this connection to the Winter Court. Was it because Fae didn't suffer from the cold or was it my powers over ice that bonded me here? I shook my head and pulled the curtains closed. Brandon would suffer from the cold though. He'd already suffered enough.

See this was another reason we wouldn't be more than acquaintances. We were too different. Once we returned to Earth, we'd separate, and I'd make sure to never see him again so he wouldn't tempt me to experience the orgasms he'd promised. Many orgasms, I reminded myself. Thank goodness I'd never experienced a Fae heat otherwise I might take him up on his offer like the way Saoirse had used human men in heat knowing they wouldn't get her pregnant.

I strode over to the armoire and wrenched open the doors. An assortment of clothes lined the interior. I already grasped the layout because I'd watched a servant place the garments inside while Brandon had been unconscious. That was another thing. He was too vulnerable. Mortal. He wouldn't live long. What if I fell in love with him and then lost him the way Briana had lost her first chosen mate? She'd suffered from a broken heart for years because of it. I didn't want to be like her. When I loved, I wanted it to be a forever love.

There was no way I'd separate sex and love. That wasn't in me. When I finally gave my body to a man, it would be with my heart too. My emotions entwined my body and heart.

The running water stopped, and I creaked open the door and shoved the clothes through the gap knowing the bathtub lay on the other side of the door and I wouldn't accidentally glimpse Brandon naked.

But Dia, I wanted to. I longed to see all of him. To have all of him. I clicked the door shut and strode to the bed. Unable to help myself, I lifted a pillow and placed it under my nose to inhale the masculine scent that was all Brandon. A sharp tang of dark vanilla and earthy tones.

The things I wanted from the human... but I couldn't have them.

Footsteps sounded outside the main door, then the jangle of keys, the distinctive click of the lock popping open, and the heavy door swung inwards. I'd felt like a prisoner even though Tay said it was for our protection. Tay stood on the other side of the door. Her gaze flickered to the pillow in my hands, so I quickly tossed it on the bed as heat rushed into my face.

Tay's gaze slid around the room assessing. I'd watched her do it many times as though she was taking many pictures in her mind to examine later.

"He's awake I see," she said.

"Aye."

"A servant will be back to escort you both to dinner in an hour." With that declaration, she shut the door and locked it again.

I slumped onto the bed. What did the demons want from us? And would we ever get home?

CHAPTER NINE
BRANDON

ROISIN'S DAINTY HAND FLUNG the clothes in so quickly that if I'd blinked, I would have missed it. I lowered myself into the large claw-footed bathtub and slid my head under the water. Had I blown it already with her? The words had just slipped out as though I was a randy teenager about to get my first blowjob. I was way cooler than this, but she had my insides tied up in knots and I couldn't think straight around her the longer I was with her.

Shifting up the bathtub, my head broke the surface of the water. My gaze stared at the stone ceiling. I assumed it was a castle since the room we were in was so opulent and large. The thing that struck me though was there was only one bed in the room, and I'd been lying in it. Did that mean Roisin hadn't slept? Or had she slept beside me? That thought made my cock hard yet again.

Wrapping my hand around the length, I ran my palm up and down imagining Roisin's pretty pink lips stretched around my dick. Maybe this was all I should have of her. A vivid imagination of the Fae Princess who had captured my heart in the palms of her dainty hands. I grunted, holding in my groan, so she didn't hear me relieving the tension inside me. My palm swept over the weeping tip of my cock as my hips thrust up out of the water. I used my pre-cum as a lubricant and fantasized about spreading Roisin's legs and gathering her arousal to mix with my own. My hand worked faster. How she'd be so wet for me that my fingers would slide into her. How she'd beg for my cock instead, but I'd make her wait until she was on the very edge of orgasm before giving her the hard length of my cock.

And then as I pushed into her welcoming wet heat, she'd beg me to make her mine, and I would. My hand worked faster now imagining I was claiming Roisin. How I'd pin her legs wide and stroke her clit with my slick fingers as she convulsed around my cock.

My release came out in a sudden force, shocking me with its surge and strength. Streams jetted over my chest and hit my chin in a warm splatter. Another tug on my cock and more seeped from the tip.

I'd never come so hard in my life. Maybe now I'd stop pushing her to admit she wanted me as much as I wanted her because I couldn't stop thinking about us together. It was an obsession. She was my obsession.

Imagine what it'd be like if I was doing all those things to Roisin.

A loud knock pounded on the door.

"Hurry in there. They're taking us out of the room to dinner."

I dropped my hips back under the water and cleared my throat.

"They?"

"Tay stopped by. She didn't say who."

Well, shit, we were about to meet the rest of the demons and I'd covered myself in my release. I reached for the washcloth.

While I'd been washing and dressing, and jerking off, Roisin had changed clothes. She stood in the center of the room in a dress so regal, it was made for royalty. The fabric was an opulent gold that shone from the flames at her back. It almost gave her a halo effect and if I'd been dreaming, I would have called her an angel.

Fae Princess in all her splendid glory. Way out of my league. The Fellowship had trained me to protect the Fae and not seduce them, so why was that my only thought for Roisin?

"You look beautiful, but then you always do," I said, striding across the room to be closer to her.

A moth to the flame came to mind. Would she burn me up? Reduce me to ash? I doubted it since she appeared hesitant to do anything with me at all.

"You don't look too bad." She ran an assessing eye over my attire.

The pants were snug as though the designer had made them for someone less muscular than me, but the material was a soft black I hadn't experienced before. When I'd first seen the Fae attire, I had thought little about the differences in the material, but now wearing demon attire, the differences touched my skin in a sensual slide of fabric. The shirt was a shimmering green and blue material that reminded me of the Northern Lights. It made me feel otherworldly and cemented the fact we were in another world far away from the people I loved.

What must my mother and grandfather be thinking about my disappearance? And Roisin's disappearance? Would they blame the Fae? Or would the Fae blame us humans for Roisin disappearing?

"What's wrong?" she asked.

"What makes you assume something is wrong?"

She pointed at my face. "The deep scowl between your eyebrows."

I let out a long breath. "I was wondering what everyone back home was thinking about us disappearing and if they were blaming each other."

A dainty scowl tugged at her blonde eyebrows. "I hope not. We need to get back so that doesn't happen."

"Agreed. We can't lose the Fae from Earth again. We need them to fix it."

Her lips pursed.

"What?"

"Is that all we're good for?"

"I'm sure you're good for many things." I winked, my mind once again returning to us in bed, or out of it. Hell, anywhere.

She huffed but a light pink stained her cheeks. All her blushing made me consider she might be a virgin, but surely not when she was fifty years old. Even if Fae aged differently, fifty was still a lot of years to have lived and not experienced sex.

I wanted to ask her.

A knock pounded on the door, then the key clanged in the ancient lock before the heavy wooden door swung inwards.

"Come with me," a demon with long straight black horns said.

I'd never seen her before, but Roisin nodded and walked from the room. Had she met this demon before? Did she trust her? I wasn't game to trust anyone here. Why would they have made a portal to this realm in our sacred library? And how?

CHAPTER TEN
ROISIN

I SENSED BRANDON'S PRESENCE at my back. It sent fluttering tingles of awareness over my skin. The low cut of the dress at the back barely covered my rear end. It was like I detected Brandon's eyes on my naked skin. What would his fingers be like running up my back?

The demon in front turned her head and stared over her shoulder at me. The black depths of her eyes were like bottomless pits. I stumbled forward a step, but Brandon clasped my waist with his firm hands and kept me upright. The demon's forked tongue flicked out to her lips like a snake scenting the air. She grinned, then turned back around.

Goosebumps danced over my skin. Brandon's thumbs swiped across my lower back teasing the bare skin. A shudder ran through my entire body as desire pooled between my legs.

"You can let go now," I said tipping my chin up in the air and forcing myself to sound normal.

His warm breath shifted closer to my ear. "I'll protect you from everything."

The gust of his voice so close sent another shiver down my neck and made my nipples pebble. At least this dress wasn't sheer like the other one, plus my back was to him. I almost leaned back into him, but I shook myself out of the lust bouncing between us and slapped his hands.

"Even your own feet." He let go with a chuckle.

The warmth of his breath and body disappeared making me wish he was right back where he was. I'd been stronger with him holding me which was ridiculous since I was a powerful Fae Princess, and he was human.

We continued walking along the castle hallways. They were nothing like the ones in the Summer Court palace. These were dark gray stone walls, lit by flickering orange torches on wall sconces at regular intervals. On the walls hung strange paintings of murky black and light gray, lines, symbols, and strange-looking handprints in dark red etched on the canvases. I longed to stop and study the artwork more so I might decipher the symbols which is what Ciara would have thought about.

"Here we are." The demon stopped outside a set of double wooden doors. She tapped her knuckles on the wood and the doors swung inward as if by magic.

Tay sat at a circular table, a shiny black cloth beneath the glistening silver plates. In the center of the table was a three-tiered platter laden with food.

"Come in and sit." She waved her hand at the empty chairs opposite her.

The demon closed the door behind us and with no other option, I walked over to the table. Brandon rushed to my side and pulled the chair out. I sat and fluffed the long skirts of the dress around my legs. Brandon took the empty seat next to me. Purple curtains hung from the windows, and they were open to the snowy scene outside. Above our heads dangled a black chandelier lit by flickering candles. The mantle over the fireplace was the same as the one in the bedroom we were occupying, but this one had a mirror above it.

"Cozy," he said, glancing around the room like a guard taking in all the threats, but it was only us three in the room.

"I wanted to become better acquainted with our guests," Tay said, lifting a silver goblet to her lips and sipping whatever liquid she had inside.

"Guests isn't the right word, is it?" Brandon asked.

Tay shrugged. I glanced around the room. There were more of the strange paintings hanging in here as well. A fire crackled in the open fireplace, but the flames were purple, and they cast a strange glow over Tay. Everything in the room pulsed with magic.

"We've treated you kindly, so yes, guests is the right word."

"You're keeping us prisoner, locked up in a room."

"Purely for your protection." She slammed the goblet on the table spilling red droplets down the side of the silver and onto the black tablecloth. The liquid seeped into the fabric.

"What do we need protecting from?" I asked, calmly, trying to diffuse the tension building between the two.

Tay's dark gaze landed on me. "You're a Fae Princess, so a lot."

"We don't have enemies any longer. The Trappers are all dead. I don't understand how you believe we have enemies."

"You're right." She dabbed her finger on the damp tablecloth and then touched it to her lips.

Brandon and I exchanged a glance. The demon was acting crazy or was this how demons acted?

"How did we get here?" I asked.

"You comprehend how you got here," she said. "Through the bookshelf."

"But no one else has come through the bookshelf. They've only taken books."

Her eyebrows rose high on her head. "I'll have to talk to my brother about that."

"You have a brother?"

"Two. Both kings. Meanwhile, I'm a princess like you."

"I have two brothers, too."

We shared a knowing smile. I loved Rian and Lorcan, but they were overbearing sometimes.

"We didn't mean to come here. Can you help us return to Earth?"

Tay picked up a small velvet pouch and pulled out a handful of trinkets, ranging from stones to feathers, and even what looked like bone. She shook them in her hand.

"You didn't mean to, but you came here. Everything happens for a reason." She tossed the trinkets onto the liquid-stained tablecloth.

The items settled into a pattern, reminding me of the paintings on her walls. I stared at the stones, feathers, and bone, then at the paintings.

"You painted all of those?"

Tay nodded while tapping a long, sharp fingernail to each stone.

"The brushwork is amazing."

Her head snapped up. "You paint?"

"Aye. It's my favorite pastime. Flowers, the palace, library... but nothing like yours." I stood and walked to the closest painting. "I've seen nothing like it."

"Of course not." She scoffed. "Demon magic."

"The painting is magic?" I lifted my hand.

"Don't touch them," she snapped.

Before I lowered my hand, Brandon was by my side placing his hand over mine as though he was prepared to take the brunt of whatever magic was about to harm me, but he was human and who knows how bad it would hurt him.

"What were you thinking?" I asked.

"Stopping you from touching another magical thing that might take you away for all we comprehend."

Tay laughed. "No portals here unless I create one."

"So, you're saying the bookshelf wasn't a portal."

"No." She scowled.

I returned to the table and sat.

"Why would your brother bring me here?"

She stared at the items again. "Unless..."

Half a second later, her hand snapped out taking mine in her palm. She dragged it across the table until it hovered over the odd trinkets. I half expected something magical to happen, but nothing did. She pressed her thumbnail into the soft flesh of my wrist.

"Stop it." I tugged on my hand, but her grip was strong.

"Just one drop," she whispered.

"Let go," Brandon said storming across the room.

But her nail popped the tender skin, and blood dripped onto the items beneath me. The blood sizzled and sparked as though trying to make a fire. Tay let go of my hand just as Brandon reached my side. I snatched my arm back and cradled it against my chest. The prick from her nail hurt, but I was more shocked than anything that she'd made me bleed.

"Are you all right?" Brandon asked.

I nodded my head. He turned to Tay, his expression murderous. I grabbed him with both hands, stopping him. His gaze dropped to my bleeding wrist.

Tay's voice echoed throughout the room as she mumbled incoherent words. Was she speaking another language?

Her gaze snapped to mine. "You." Then she smiled so happily that it made the scene even more bizarre.

CHAPTER ELEVEN
BRANDON

"**I**'M GETTING YOU OUT of here," I said.

Roisin's fingers tightened on me. The sight of her bleeding made me want to murder the demon who'd made her bleed. I picked up a napkin and dabbed at the wound, but the skin had already healed underneath the blood and all that remained was a tiny pink pin prick mark. At least that was something, but what did the demon do with her blood? What spell did she make? Were we stuck here forever?

"You can go back to your room now." Tay clicked her fingers, and the door swung open.

The demon who'd escorted us here stood on the other side waiting.

"Not until you tell us why you hurt Roisin."

"Is she hurt?" Tay asked lifting her head from staring at the items for so long it was like they'd hypnotized her.

"That's beside the point. You hurt her."

"We're immortal, little human. We heal quickly from a slight wound. We'd heal from even larger wounds, unlike you who'd die. Don't test my patience. I said leave." She pointed at the door.

Roisin tugged my biceps. I wanted answers, but my job was to protect Roisin, and what a shit job I'd done so far.

"Fine," I spat. "Don't believe this is the end."

Tay smiled creepily. "This is so much more than the end."

I let Roisin pull me toward the door mainly because she was touching me, and I didn't want her to stop. The second we were through the door, it slammed shut.

"That was creepy."

Roisin wrapped her arm through mine as though I was escorting her to a formal dance. I didn't mind in the least because it kept her close to me and touching me.

"Why would she make you bleed on all those bizarre objects?"

"Magic I'm assuming," Roisin said. "I should have read more books like Ciara instead of painting. Not a very useful pastime for me to do."

"Never give up what you love." I stepped closer to her, so our hips brushed with each step along the long castle hallway.

"Have you?"

I tapped my finger against my leg. Had I?

"No. If you love painting don't stop for anyone or anything."

We arrived back at the bedroom. The demon unlocked the door and waited for us to enter. How would we ever get out of here? They kept us under lock and key. Our captor might be crazy, and the bookshelf wasn't a portal, so even if we went searching, we wouldn't find a way home. My guess was the demons made the portals themselves. It was entirely different from the Veil between the Fae Kingdom and Earth. How I longed to be back home with the stuff I was familiar with.

Roisin hesitated on the threshold of the room as though she too was undecided if we should go back into the room. A tiny exhale made her chest deflate, dragging my gaze back to her breasts. At least in the demon's presence, I'd had the wits about me to stop staring at Roisin, but now we were about to be alone, I didn't have the willpower to keep from staring at her beauty.

She walked inside the bedroom with me by her side. As predicted, the demon closed the door behind us and locked it.

"Well, this sucks," I said. "I didn't eat a thing and I'm hungry."

Roisin laughed, her entire body shaking beside mine. She slid her arm out of our cozy nook and walked over to the fireplace. The loss of our physical connection was instantaneous. She lifted her hands toward the flames and turned them a few different ways as though searching for something.

I walked over to her and grabbed the hand the demon had stabbed with her nail.

"The mark is gone."

"Of course."

"I wanted to rip her head off for hurting you."

Roisin's pretty blue and indigo-rimmed eyes lifted. Her gaze dashed over every inch of my face.

"I saw that. I'm not sure that will kill a demon, are you?"

"No, but it'd slow her down for a bit at least."

She smiled. "It was a tiny wound."

"Any wound on you is too big."

She gazed at me as if she longed for my kiss. Was I projecting my desire onto her?

"Well," she said, tugging her hand out of mine and walking to the door. "Should we try to escape?"

"How?"

"Next time they open the door, you rip their head off, then we'll run for it through a castle no doubt full of other demons, but you can rip their heads off too, then we'll run out into the snow where you'll freeze to death."

"Roisin, are you being sarcastic?"

She rolled her eyes.

I laughed so hard it took away the last of the anger I had at the demon for hurting Roisin. I couldn't explain this overprotective urge I had for her. Sure, I was a member of the Fellowship, and it was my duty to protect the Fae. I'd grown up all my life hearing about the Fae from my mother and grandfather. About how we were the special chosen ones to keep their secrets, protect them from harm, and help them in any way they needed. But this was Roisin. The exquisite, very alluring, Roisin. The one woman in existence who made my heart thump in my chest and made me forget all my years of training, for who I was. Whenever I was near her, there was only her. My need to please her. Protect her in a way that had nothing to do with being a Fellowship member and everything to do with being a man who'd developed feelings for a woman.

The door opened, making Roisin startle back a few steps. Four demons walked inside, one carrying a tray of food, the other a jug and a tray of goblets, the next with paints, the last with a canvas. They didn't say a word to us but set the trays on the small tables next to the chairs by the fireplace, and the canvas and paints by the window. They'd left the door wide open, but Roisin didn't even look at the door to escape and I was too far away. While I might have thought I'd try to take on one horned demon, four might be a bit of a stretch. Okay, a lot probably since they were all taller than me and I wasn't short at six foot four.

They left as quickly as they'd come.

"I guess you won't go hungry after all," Roisin said.

"Come here and let's eat."

I watched her walk toward me, her gaze flickering between me and the canvas. It was like an intangible thread pulled her toward the art tools. I saw the love for it in her eyes. I'd do anything to have her look at me that way, too.

She sat in the ornate seat, so I sat in the other one opposite her, not used to such decadent furniture.

"This looks delicious," she said.

"Smells it too." I handed her a small plate. "After you, Princess."

"I'm not sure my title means much here."

"You're wrong." I picked up a handful of blueberries and placed them on her plate. "The demon princess respected you were a princess, too."

"How can you be sure?"

I tapped the side of my nose as I grinned. "My training. Plus, it was obvious with the way she talked to you."

"I suppose I'm familiar with people talking to me that way." She smiled. "How did you realize I liked blueberries?"

"Everyone knows Fae love blueberries."

I picked a few pieces of cured meat from the other side of the tray and placed them on my plate. I'd need all the sustenance I could get if we were to figure out a way out of here.

"And you, what do you love?"

I caught and held her gaze. 'You' hovered on the tip of my tongue, but I couldn't love her. I barely knew her.

"Tell me about the Summer Court."

"What would you like to know?"

"Everything," I said. It was true. I wanted to learn everything about her. About what else she loved. If she might ever love me?

CHAPTER TWELVE

ROISIN

I TALKED FOR HOURS with Brandon about my home and family. The words came from my mouth in a flow of never-ending love for them all. After I hesitated to talk to him on Earth, I was at such ease around him we could have been together forever. The flickering flames from the fireplace cast alluring shadows over his handsome face as he sat eating the food one piece at a time, as though enthralled by my voice. If I didn't know any better, I'd say my voice was like Mothers where she influenced us to a small extent with her singing. I sang little over the years, but when I had, there was no effect like when my mother sang. She was truly special, and she made all her children feel special, too.

Brandon stopped eating and curled into the chair, a deep yawn stretched his masculine jaw. The sharp edges drew my gaze to the painting easel set up by the window. My fingers itched to paint him. As I talked, his eyelids lowered, his breathing grew heavy, and soon he was asleep. Should I be offended my talking put him to sleep or happy he was comfortable in my presence to fall asleep?

I stared at his handsome face for a long time as I had for the last few days waiting for him to wake. At least this time he was only sleeping, and I didn't have to worry that he might not wake. I frowned. At least I hoped he had healed. Since he was a human, I couldn't be too sure, but Tay had been rather kind while she'd worked on him. She was abrupt, but I assumed that was her demeanor. Tonight with her had been strange. Those bizarre items she'd pulled from her pouch were even more strange. And why did she make me bleed over them?

I didn't understand her demon magic.

While they had us locked in this room, I'd never discover anything to help us. I strode over to the door and tried the door handle. It didn't budge. I kicked the bottom of the door, then cursed under my breath at the throb in my big toe.

My gaze snagged on the easel. I suppose there wasn't anything else for me to do. Brandon was sleeping soundly in the chair, the firelight flickered softly over his still face. Dia, he was even more alluring like this. What would happen if I snuck over there and placed a tiny kiss on his unsuspecting lips?

I shook my head. It was like I was in a daze whenever I looked at Brandon. I strode over to the easel and set to work. Soft music hummed from my throat as I worked with the paints, mixing colors and stroking the softest of brushes over the canvas. Each dab of color added another element to the painting and soon I was so entranced by my process that I almost had the entire image of Brandon sleeping painted before he woke.

He woke lazily, stretching his arms above his head and drawing my gaze to the thick muscles of his biceps. Brandon appeared strong enough to fling me over his shoulder and carry me away. I almost laughed aloud at that thought. His eyes fluttered open and snagged on my face as though he, too, experienced the attraction between us. My breath paused for a beat as though he'd caught me doing something I shouldn't.

His lips kicked up at the corners. "What are you up to over there?"

"Painting." I waved my paintbrush in the air. Drops of pastel pink paint fell onto my dress. The pink I'd been using to paint his lips and daydreaming about kissing again while doing it. My cheeks heated.

His eyes narrowed. "What are you painting?"

"Nothing," I said, reaching for the nearest item to cover the painting, but there was nothing in reach.

He stood and walked toward me. My blush intensified. I stood and spread my arms.

"You can't look."

"Why not?"

"It's not finished."

"So?"

He stepped around the easel, so I spun quickly, keeping my arms wide and trying my best to cover the painting. Brandon leaned left, and so did I. He leaned right, and so did I.

"You're making this difficult."

"Good."

He was so close that I saw his nostrils flare. A second later, his firm hands landed on my waist, then he lifted me off my feet, spun us around, and put me down. I gasped, but he'd turned back to the painting.

"That wasn't fair," I said, while my body was running wild with arousal at his touch. The way he'd lifted me sent my heart into overdrive.

"It wasn't fair of you painting me while I slept." He kept his back to me.

Suddenly I was unsure of my painting when I always recognized people loved them. Had I painted him in the hopes he'd love it?

"I mean, my eyes are closed, and I'm wearing clothes. How about next time I be naked with my eyes open?" He turned around and gave me a saucy smile.

"What?" I gasped the word.

"I'd like that. Wouldn't you?"

"I... I'm..."

He chuckled. "Does that mean you haven't painted nudes?"

My cheeks flamed. "No."

"Good. I'll be your first."

"Brandon. No." I shook my head. "I don't do those sorts of paintings."

"Pity." He shrugged. "You'd be exceptional at it, but then you already are an amazing painter. This is good. It'd hang in one of our art galleries and thousands of people would admire it."

"You're only saying that because you like the thought of it being you hanging in an art gallery." I dropped the paintbrush into the tin of cleaning solution.

"I look good." He smirked.

"I should have painted something else. I'll never hear the end of this, will I?"

"Maybe... unless you tell me why you painted me."

"There wasn't much else to paint." I waved my hand around the room.

Brandon reached over my shoulder. My body flared with instant awareness. Was he going to touch me? But he wrenched open the curtain behind my back. Sunlight spilled into the room, breaking the cozy atmosphere of us being secluded. Alone.

"I guess this snow-covered wonderland outside wasn't much else?" He raised an eyebrow.

He was so close that if I raised onto my tiptoes, I'd kiss him. I couldn't even look away from him to see the scene outside the window, but I understood from days of staring at the Winter Court that it was indeed a magical scene and one worthy of painting.

I licked my lips because words were failing me now. His eyes flared as they tracked the motion. Every inch of my body stilled for a heartbeat, then I pushed past him.

"I need to wash up. I have paint everywhere."

An embarrassing wave of heat washed over me. I dashed across the room and shoved the bathing chamber door shut. One glance in the mirror showed my bright red face. What a hideous sight. Whenever I was around Brandon, he made my emotions go all over the place. How would I keep denying our attraction while the demons had us trapped in a room together?

CHAPTER THIRTEEN

ROISIN

AFTER WASHING THE PAINT from my body, I opened the door with a creak.

"Brandon?" I called through the tiny gap.

"Yes?"

"Can you pass me a clean dress, please?"

"Or you can come out here naked and get it yourself. I won't complain."

I slammed the door shut. Could I stay in the bathing chambers forever? A second later, a light knock sounded on the door.

"I was only joking. I have a dress for you."

Standing behind the door, I creaked it open enough for Brandon to put his hand through. The dress he was holding dangled from his fingers.

"Thank you."

I clasped the dress and tugged it from his hand. As soon as he pulled his hand back, I shut the door and put on the dress. It was a lovely garment of the silkiest material in a deep plum color. Hauling in a centering breath, I opened the door and crossed the room to the bed.

"I'm tired."

I climbed into the bed and pulled the covers up to my chin. My hair was still damp, but I didn't care about the cooling tresses on the pillow. The warmth from the fire would dry my hair while I slept.

"Roisin?"

"Hmm?" I murmured, so tired that my eyes stayed shut and my head was heavy with the need for sleep.

"Did you sleep at all while I was unconscious?"

"No," I whispered, and then sleep claimed me.

"How long was I out for?"

"Too long," I murmured.

I woke to Brandon's warm hand gently shaking my shoulder.

"Time to wake up, Princess."

I rubbed a hand over my tired eyes.

"They've requested us to dine with them."

"Who?" I mumbled, still trying to return to the land of the wakeful.

"Tay I'm assuming. There's a guard or servant, whatever she is, at the door who came to fetch us."

"Have I been asleep that long?" I sat up.

Brandon's gaze dipped to my chest for a fleeting second.

"I'm not sure. The entire time has been daylight. It's so confusing having no night."

"Time moves differently here too, like in the Summer Court."

"That would make sense." He stepped back from the bed. "Do you need a moment before we leave?"

I glanced over at the door and then nodded. What was going to happen now? Our last invitation to dinner had been a strange event where we hadn't even eaten. Was Tay about to cut me again? Make me bleed on bizarre items?

"I don't want to go," I whispered.

Everything inside me said to stay here with Brandon.

"Me either," he whispered back. "But we won't find a way out stuck in here."

I nodded. He was right. Even if I didn't want to leave the relative safety of the room, we had to. I tossed back the blankets and strode to the armoire. I pulled out a wrinkle-free dress and carried it into the bathing chambers. There I changed quickly. The sooner we found a way out, the better.

Returning to Brandon, he walked over to the door and knocked on it. The door opened and the demon from last time stood waiting for us.

"This way."

We followed her through the grand castle once again, but this time she took us a different way. I suppose that meant we were going to an unfamiliar room, which was good. It meant we'd learn more about the layout of the castle. Hopefully, I'd find a way to escape.

She strode up to a set of double wooden doors and opened them. She dipped in a bow as we walked past her and into the enormous dining hall. A long, black wooden table stretched from one end to the other. High-backed black wooden chairs lined the sides. At the end sat a throne-like chair. For the King, I assumed. Just as Father had a more special chair in the Summer Court. The room was empty except for us.

"Now what?" Brandon asked.

"We wait." I smoothed the skirts of my dress.

"For?"

"Our hosts." I refrained from rolling my eyes like Briana always did at inane questions.

"Do we sit?"

"Dia, no. What did they teach you in that school of yours? It certainly wasn't manners."

"I love it when you get sassy with me." He stepped closer. "It means I'm getting to you."

"Annoying me." I huffed.

"I don't think so, Princess."

As I folded my arms over my chest, I said, "What would you call it, then?"

"Attraction. Desire. Sexual tension. You're frustrated and I can help." He stepped closer still. "How about if we survive this dinner, you give me five minutes to ease the tension for you?"

"Five minutes?" I stepped backward. "From what my sisters say, it should be hours."

"So, you are a virgin?"

"I never said that," I said, flustered.

"You don't have to, sweetheart. It's your body. Your choice."

He stepped forward, and I stepped backward until my back met the wall. The stones were warm against my bare back.

"But if it's hours you want, then I'll give you hours. Anything you want from me and it's yours."

I poked my finger into his chest to stop him from coming any closer, but the second I connected with his body, my body had other ideas and my fingers curled into the firmness of his chest. "Not happening," I stuttered. Then shored myself up against his allure. "You can promise all you like, but you'll never be my fated mate."

"You intend to wait forever to have sex?"

"I'll wait forever to be happy with the man destined for me."

"You break my heart, Roisin." He placed his hands over his chest, knocking my finger aside.

"You're being dramatic. You don't love me."

He smirked. "Guess you'll never know."

I tossed my hair back over my shoulder. "You can't possibly love me."

"Can't I?" The look he gave me grew heavier each second we stared at one other.

"No, because you don't even know me."

"I know enough. I know you love painting and your eyes light up with happiness every time you look at art or even think about making art. You love your family more than anything in the world and you'd do everything in your power to protect them. Sweet Roisin, you believe in forever love... the type of love everyone wants. You're kind and caring, even when in the most extreme circumstances. You hold yourself with grace and poise. Your smile could light a thousand suns and fuel a thousand realms."

No one had ever said such beautiful words to me. Did he love me? Mother and Father had fallen in love the day they met, but they were fated mates, so their love was destined. What Brandon and I felt for each other was different. It was desire and lust, nothing more. It wasn't love. Perhaps I should kiss him, even have sex with him, to prove it was nothing but sexual tension between us, and that's all it would ever be. But what if it was more?

Loud voices erupted in the room.

"Rexan, listen to me," Tay said.

Tay spotted us and stopped in her tracks. The hulking demon beside her stopped, too.

"You sense it, don't you, brother?" Tay asked.

The demon grunted. Dia, he was enormous. Easily over seven feet tall, and that wasn't measuring the horns on top of his head. They were broad and set amongst a thick mane of black hair.

"Fuck," he said.

"Yeah," Tay said.

"I guess the time has come."

Tay nodded and resumed walking toward us. I couldn't go back any further than I wanted to. Their intimidating walk in our direction made me want to flee, but Brandon stood between me and the two demons.

"What do you want with the Princess?" Brandon asked.

The male demon, Rexan, ran his dark gaze over him.

"How did the human get here?" he asked Tay, ignoring Brandon's question.

"He came with the Fae Princess."

"Interesting." He tapped his lip with a clawed finger.

"One of you needs to talk, or I'm taking the Princess and leaving."

Tay and Rexan exchanged a look, then roared with laughter.

"Come on, Roisin. I'm getting you out of here."

"Where do you assume you'll go, weak human?" Tay asked. "You almost died the moment you stepped foot in our realm."

I placed a hand on Brandon's shoulder. Tay was right. We wouldn't get out of here alive if we didn't play nicely with the demons.

"I apologize for my guard," I said, stepping around Brandon. "He hasn't received the best training with the Fellowship, and I'll fix that the moment we return to Earth."

"You came from Earth?" Rexan asked.

"Aye."

"The Fae have returned to Earth to rule?"

"That has yet to be decided by the King."

Rexan gave me a grim smile. "Please, where are my manners? I'm the Demon King. Since we're family, you may call me Rexan in private. This is my sister, Tay."

"Family?" I asked.

"Ah, young princess, there is quite a tale to be told. Please have a seat and we will talk over a meal."

I walked toward the closest chair, my legs so shaky I didn't believe I'd make it there in time before I collapsed. Luckily for me, Brandon pulled the chair out and pushed it in, then he sat beside me and found my hand under the table. The warmth of his hand was comforting over mine. There was more to the connection between Brandon and me. We weren't simply a princess and her bodyguard. We weren't a Fae and a human, but I couldn't concentrate on my feelings for Brandon now. Not after what the Demon King said.

How in all the realms was I family with the Demon King?

CHAPTER FOURTEEN
ROISIN

THE DEMON KING TOOK his seat in the throne-like chair made for his colossal size. Beside him sat two larger chairs than the rest, suggesting they too were crafted for the enormous size of these demons. As it was, the ornately carved black wood chairs we were sitting in were too big, but that was the least of my concerns.

I opened my mouth to ask questions, but servers entered the room in a stream carrying never-ending plates of food. They piled them on the table as though there would be twenty people joining us.

"Are others coming?" I asked.

"No," the Demon King said.

"So much food..."

"The plates in front of you are all vegetarian."

I raised my head, surprised by the fact the Demon King realized Fae were vegetarians.

"You're well versed in Fae needs." I spooned a helping onto my plate.

"I'm well versed in everyone's needs. It's what demons do."

Brandon choked on the food in his mouth.

"Problem, human?"

Brandon shook his head. "Humans believe demons are evil and they try to take our souls."

"Humans don't realize the truth."

"What is the truth?"

"Do you trust this man, Princess Roisin?"

I glanced at Brandon's profile. I hadn't been with him long, and while he liked to test my boundaries, there was no malicious harm to Brandon. He'd trained for years to protect Fae. He'd tried protecting me as best as possible in these bizarre circumstances. There was nothing he'd done to not gain my trust except push me to acknowledge the attraction between us, and that was more of a man and woman thing.

"I do."

"We may speak freely around him? I have a lot of sensitive knowledge to share with you."

"You may. If he breaks my trust, then..." I trailed off, knowing I'd have to kill him. Did I have it in me to kill a human? My father and brother had killed the Trappers. Of course I had it in me to eliminate any threat to my family. "I'll be the one to punish him."

Brandon's eyes widened as though he didn't expect me to have a brutal side. He didn't understand me at all. He saw me as the pretty virgin princess he'd charm into bed. I wasn't naïve even if everyone thought I was. And while I liked to paint, I too, had trained with swords and other various fighting methods. Father was determined we'd always be able to protect ourselves.

"Demons take human memories when they barter with us to portal to other realms," Rexan said.

"What do demons want with human memories?" Brandon asked.

"They're fuel for a better word," Tay said.

"Sustenance," Rexan said with a slight smile.

"That too." Tay grinned.

"We take no one's soul."

"Perhaps humans can argue their soul is made from memories and feelings," I said. "And that you're feeding from them."

"One could," Rexan said, not denying my claim.

He stabbed his fork into a bloody piece of meat and ate it. I looked down at my plate.

"What does this have to do with me being family to *you*? My father is from the original Fae royal lineage. My mother is from Fae on Earth."

Rexan placed his fork on the table. "I agree. Your father's lineage is impeccable. Your mother's, on the other hand..."

"What about my mother?"

I sat up straighter as ice covered my hands. No one would talk ill of my mother. She was the sweetest, most caring person in our court.

"Your mother knows part of her history is steeped in Sirens."

"No." I gasped.

"True."

"You're only saying that because you like the thought of it being you hanging in an art gallery." I dropped the paintbrush into the tin of cleaning solution.

"I look good." He smirked.

"I should have painted something else. I'll never hear the end of this, will I?"

"Maybe... unless you tell me why you painted me."

"There wasn't much else to paint." I waved my hand around the room.

Brandon reached over my shoulder. My body flared with instant awareness. Was he going to touch me? But he wrenched open the curtain behind my back. Sunlight spilled into the room, breaking the cozy atmosphere of us being secluded. Alone.

"I guess this snow-covered wonderland outside wasn't much else?" He raised an eyebrow.

He was so close that if I raised onto my tiptoes, I'd kiss him. I couldn't even look away from him to see the scene outside the window, but I understood from days of staring at the Winter Court that it was indeed a magical scene and one worthy of painting.

I licked my lips because words were failing me now. His eyes flared as they tracked the motion. Every inch of my body stilled for a heartbeat, then I pushed past him.

"I need to wash up. I have paint everywhere."

An embarrassing wave of heat washed over me. I dashed across the room and shoved the bathing chamber door shut. One glance in the mirror showed my bright red face. What a hideous sight. Whenever I was around Brandon, he made my emotions go all over the

"Humans believe demons lie," Brandon said. "What's saying you're not lying now?"

Rexan sighed. "Ask her yourself then."

"I will." I shoved back my chair and stood. "And how do you fit in with this?"

"She's part Rage Demon, too."

I fell back into the chair. "You're saying I'm part Siren, part Rage Demon, part Fae?"

"Yes. And what a charming combination you are." He nodded at my hands.

"I don't believe you. Why wouldn't Mother have told us? Father too?"

"I doubt your father knows. As for your mother, she made a deal with Saltine. You'd have to talk to those two to learn the specifics."

"Saltine, the witch seer?"

He scoffed. "She's more than a witch seer, young princess."

"Are you my great grandfather then?"

"No, I'm your great, not sure how many, uncle."

I turned to Tay. "So, you're my great grandmother?"

Tay huffed out a laugh. "Aunty."

"Who am I directly related to then?" I scowled.

Tay placed her hand on her brother's arm. "Shouldn't they be the ones to tell them?"

Rexan inclined his head, his thick hair ruffling against his horns as he did so. "You're right, sister. I've already sent doves to them."

"Doves?" Brandon asked.

Rexan and Tay ignored his question. The doves were the least of my concerns after the imploding information that kept going off inside my head. I wasn't entirely Fae. Siren and Demon blood ran through my veins.

"How?"

They both looked at me.

"How do you know I'm related to you?"

"Rage demons sense each other. We're more powerful than other demons. It's why we're the rulers of the Winter Court," Tay said. "We sensed you the moment you stepped into our realm, and I made certain last night when I checked your blood."

"I sense nothing." I shook my head. At least I now comprehended why she'd made me bleed on those strange items, and she wouldn't be doing it again.

"You're young," Tay said.

I'd had enough of everyone calling me young. With a calmness I didn't have, I said, "I'd like to leave now."

"Of course, you'll head back and return with your mother. I understand you have siblings too. They're welcome to return with you," Rexan said and stood.

"I'll take you," Tay said.

"No," Rexan said. "She can return the way she came here."

"We both can," I said, glancing at Brandon.

"The human stays," Rexan said.

"Why?"

"Our guarantee you'll come back," he said.

Shite, there went our only hope to escape the Winter Court and these insane demons who thought we were related. Fae were once the guardians of Earth and humans. I'd never willingly leave a human to die in my stead. The demons were certain I'd come back for him.

But they weren't aware of my growing feelings for him. They were the reason I'd come back.

CHAPTER FIFTEEN
BRANDON

"**D**ON'T WORRY ABOUT ME," I said. "I'll be fine kicking my heels up relaxing in this fine castle."

Roisin stared at me as though I had a neon sign on my head saying crazy. I might well be, but if this was her chance to escape, then I had to let her go. It was my duty to protect the Fae. My duty to put their lives before mine. I'd do even more to keep Roisin safe.

I didn't believe a word the demons were saying. All humans grasped demons were liars. Cheaters. Soul stealers.

Get Roisin out of here. My family would be upset if I didn't return.

"Can I talk to my guard for a minute first?" Roisin asked.

Tay snapped her fingers. "The servant will return you to your room. I'll be along shortly to return you to Earth."

I stood and walked with Roisin to the open doorway where the same servant demon who'd escorted us here waited to take us back.

Our trip back to the bedroom was stone quiet. I didn't have it in me to tease Roisin, not with everything the demons had said to us. As soon as we were back in the bedroom, and the door locked behind us, I turned to her.

"Go."

"I'm not leaving you here."

"Roisin, go. This is your chance to escape. Your chance to return to your family."

"But you should come with me."

"It's your chance to find your fated mate."

She narrowed her eyes. "I can't believe you'd stoop that low."

"Why not? It's what you keep harping on about."

"I do not." She threw her hands up in the air, sending a jolt of power into the ceiling and showering us with tiny snow particles.

"Look. You'll survive outside if we try to escape. I won't. If you go back now, then you can come back and get me out of here safely. Without me freezing to death."

"You're making entirely too much sense."

I chuckled.

"You found a way here. You'll find your way back."

"But?"

"I must protect you. If me staying here does that, then you have to leave."

"Oh, Brandon." She sighed. "Your duty to the Fellowship shouldn't put my life above yours."

"Why?"

"Because all life is important, be that Fae or human, even demon."

"Roisin." I sighed her name like a plea. "They won't let me go with you, so stop arguing with me. I can study the demons while I'm here and find out if they're lying to you."

We stared at each other in a stalemate. The fire crackled as the flames danced around the room, bathing her in an ethereal glow. Even with her tiny tantrum, was she part rage demon? She was still the most beautiful woman I'd ever seen.

"If this is it for me, can you tell my mother and grandfather that I love them and that they shouldn't mourn my loss because I died doing what the Fellowship trained me for?"

"You won't give your life for mine." She strode across the room. "I won't allow it."

"Hate to say it, Princess, but we don't have a choice here."

"There's always a choice."

Her gaze flickered from my eyes down to my mouth, back up to my eyes, down to my mouth. The ever-present tension between us thrummed as though magic itself.

"I suppose if you're going to die, then I owe you a kiss."

I wanted to cheer for victory. Instead, I slid my hand to the back of her head, reveling in the way she shivered from my touch. The air hung heavier still with the desire between us. I lowered my head slowly, wanting to remember this moment forever. She'd chosen me. Chosen to kiss me. Chosen me to be her first kiss.

Well, I assumed her first kiss since she was a virgin and appeared to be saving herself for her fated mate.

Shoving that thought away, I took in the wide expanse of her eyes, staring at me with expectation and wonder. My gaze dropped to her lips. They parted as though pleading with me to take them. And I would. Lower my mouth moved until our lips hovered scant millimeters apart.

"You sense the connection too, don't you?" I whispered.

I didn't wait for her answer. My lips claimed hers. She gasped into my mouth, allowing me access to slip my tongue inside and coax hers into a melding of two souls.

This was no ordinary kiss.

It was claiming.

Demanding she was mine.

And be damned with her fated mate, wherever he might be.

Because Roisin was meant for me.

CHAPTER SIXTEEN

ROISIN

B RANDON'S KISS WAS EPIC. There was no other word
for it. Like anyone, I'd wondered what my first kiss
would be like, but I'd never dreamed of this. The way his
lips coaxed mine to move as though they were dancing
under a spell. The way his tongue stroked softly against
mine, as though he was tasting the very essence of me.
It was beautiful and made all my problems vanish into
nothing. There was only us.

I'd kiss him for an eternity, and it wouldn't be enough.

My hands clung to him as though I was afraid if I let
go, he'd vanish into a puff of air. I couldn't lose Brandon.
The notion of leaving him here made my skin crawl.

I shoved him backward. "I'm not leaving you."

He smirked. "I knew it."

"What?" I folded my arms over my heaving chest.

"I knew you felt something for me." He closed the
small distance between us and cupped my face in both
hands, then kissed me again with a gentle kiss that
seared into my heart. "I'll be here waiting for you."

"I can't go," I sobbed. The very idea of leaving him behind made my heart hurt.

"Roisin." He forced my gaze onto his. "Go."

A knock sounded on the door.

"You *have* to go now," he said.

He dropped his hands from my face and placed them on my shoulders. My entire body didn't want to move. He spun me around and marched me toward the door.

"Remember," he whispered in my ear. "I'll be here waiting for you and when you get back. I'll love you for hours like you want."

I laughed and tipped my head over my shoulder.

"Knew I'd get you to smile."

Tay opened the door with a flourish. She raised an eyebrow in question at our close embrace, but I wouldn't ignore what had happened between me and Brandon. I stepped through the door feeling the instant loss of his hands on my body. What would it be like to have him touching me, loving me, for hours? I suddenly wanted to experience it.

I said nothing because there was nothing left to say to Brandon. He comprehended I was experiencing emotions for him. Knew I'd admitted we were attracted to each other. I'd do everything in my power to get back to him and bring him home.

"I'm surprised," Tay said as we walked through the castle.

"About?"

"A lot of things actually since you arrived, but you and the human..." She shook her head. "Typically, immortals and human lovers don't last long. Mortals have such brief lives…"

"I'm well aware of that fact."

"Are you?"

"Aye."

She fell silent as the halls darkened. The wall sconces were further and further apart along this hallway, but there were more and more strange paintings.

"Why do you paint such patterns?"

Tay's dark gaze slid sideways to me. "Why do you think?"

I pursed my lips. "From what I've seen of your magic, I'd say they're spells and not simple paintings for pleasure."

A tiny bob of her head showed I'd guessed right.

"I don't believe I'm related to you."

Tay smirked. "Blood doesn't lie."

"If it's true, why didn't we know?"

Tay stopped beside a painting under the next wall sconce. The light flickered over the pattern as though pulsing.

"This one here is a protection spell." She pointed to the canvas. "I'm sure you can understand the need for such spells after what the Trappers did to the Fae."

"So, you're saying it was to protect us?"

Tay walked off. "You'll learn the whole truth when you return."

"And how am I supposed to return? I don't even understand how I got here."

Tay sighed and opened the pouch at her waist. She pulled a glowing red stone out and held it out to me.

"Take this. When you're ready to return with your family, then say the words *ira daemonium venire*. It's one use only, so don't use it until you're certain."

"*Ira daemonium venire*," I repeated.

"Yes." She stopped outside a blood-red door and handed me the stone. "We're here."

"Here?"

"The library." She sliced open her palm and placed it on the door. The door swung inwards.

Bright lights flickered into existence, illuminating the interior. Shelves upon shelves lined the room from the floor to the twenty-foot-high ceilings. Candles floated in the air at various heights. Tiny knee-high creatures darted around the room.

"What are those?"

"They're the collection demons. They collect books and store them here."

The title of the books on the nearest shelf caught my eye. I rushed over and pulled it free.

"You have all the books on the Fellowship, don't you?"

Tay shrugged.

I turned back to the shelf and gasped. Pulling another book off the shelf, I said, "And all the books on the history of the Fae."

"We did what was necessary for your protection."

"Our protection? We almost lost our immortality because we didn't have this knowledge." I hugged the books to my chest.

"You wouldn't have even been born if we hadn't stepped in." Tay yanked the books from my arms. "Be thankful for that."

"I don't understand." I huffed.

"You will once you return with your family."

I poked her in the chest with my finger. "I'm thinking humans might be right about demons that you lie and steal souls."

Tay laughed and then pushed me into the bookshelf while muttering some words. I fell backward expecting to fall into the solid shelf, but I kept falling and falling and falling until I fell on the floor landing on my bottom.

I lifted my face to the people around me, staring at me in surprise.

"Well, shite," I said. "I guess I'm back on Earth."

"Back on Earth?" Lorcan asked, holding his hand out to me.

I placed my palm in his and nodded.

"You'll never believe what I have to tell you," I said as he helped me to my feet.

"Roisin," Aislinn said, pulling me into a hug. "Where were you?"

"Would you believe the Winter Court?" I squeezed her back.

"The demon realm?" she asked, scowling.

"So, you know about it?"

"Aye, I'm older than you."

"Always with the 'older than me' comments." I rolled my eyes.

"Focus, Roisin," Lorcan said, easing Aislinn aside. "What do you have to tell us?"

A finger tapped on my arm. I glanced at the person.

"Have you seen my grandson?" Alister asked.

I gulped through the burning emotions in my throat. The guilt. The loss. The feelings I'd grown for Brandon. How had I left Brandon in the demon realm all alone?

CHAPTER SEVENTEEN

BRANDON

THE MOMENT ROISIN LEFT, it was like she'd taken a piece of me with her. I should be worried that I'd never leave the Winter Court and see my family again, but I was more worried I'd never see Roisin again. My training hadn't prepared me for the depth of feelings I'd develop for a Fae Princess.

Who knew I'd fall in love so easily?

Certainly not me.

I'd had my fair share of women, but I'd loved none of them. Guilt surged for admitting that now. Should I have taken a leaf out of Roisin's beliefs and waited for love? That's what she was waiting for. While she said it was her fated mate she was truly waiting for, then why had she kissed me? She wanted love, and by God, she had it.

I needed her to come back so I could show her how much I loved her, how much I'd love her for the rest of my mortal life. It stung like a paper cut to realize I'd die while she'd live forever. But damn it, I'd rather love her and die happy than never love her at all.

The door flung open without a knock, which was so different from the other times while Roisin was here. Did that mean the demons respected her? And now she was gone, they'd treat me differently.

Rexan, the Demon King, walked into the room as though he owned it. I suppose he did. I folded my arms over my chest.

"What do you intend to do with me?"

The King wandered the room as though a caged panther on the prowl.

"Whatever I want." He paused by the portrait Roisin had meticulously painted of me. "She is talented."

"She is."

His dark gaze snapped to mine. "She's intriguing, is she not?"

"She is," I said again.

"You might wait a while for her return."

"I'll wait forever if I have to."

"And yet you'll die." He tapped a talon on his lip. "You might even be dead before she convinces her family to come here."

"If you aim to harm her, then I'll die killing you."

The demon chuckled darkly, as though the thrill of someone trying to kill him excited him.

"You can try, but you'll never succeed where many haven't either." He strode to the doorway. "Come, it's time you learned your history."

"My history?"

The demon king strode from the room, leaving me staring at his back. Leather wings exploded in a flourish, sending a gust of air over my face. I gaped at the display of supernatural power before rushing after him. Why wasn't I powerful? We walked down a set of stairs, then another, and another. Soon a grand foyer was before us. Two guards stood at the entrance inside. They opened the door, letting in the icy chill of the winter outside. I shivered.

"I forgot." He snapped his fingers, and a guard rushed forward with a long fur cloak. "Humans are fragile."

I draped the cloak around my shoulders and tugged the hood over my head. We strode outside, our footfalls crunching on the snow. An immaculate ice-covered garden surrounded the castle. Plants that would have been spectacular in green and flower in any other place sat frozen as crystallized ice sculptures. A stone wall at waist height covered in soft-looking snow on either side of the pathway led us away from the castle. We exited the ice-sculptured garden grounds and strode across a field of ice toward the sound of loud voices and sword fighting echoing in the distance. Was he taking me to kill me already? Would my sacrifice for Roisin's life be over so quickly?

"Do other humans come here?" I asked in desperation.

"On very rare occasions. Most find it too inhospitable. We like it that way."

"Did anyone else travel through the magical bookshelf?"

"Not that I'm aware."

"It's your kingdom, so you should know."

He spun so fast, his wings almost sliced my head from my body. The talons on the tips looked sharp enough that they would do so.

"You have no sense, young man. I can snap your spine like a twig, throw you to the snow wolves roaming the forest and they'd feast on your flesh forever." The demon's eyes blazed with hunger.

I shivered despite the warmth of the fur cloak. "Let me guess, they're not like Earth wolves."

"You guessed correctly."

"My father disappeared." I shrugged. I didn't care for the man who'd abandoned me, but I'd had a fleeting thought: other people might have disappeared through the bookshelf like we had.

The demon's left eye twitched. "He might be here." His wings fluttered, sending a gust of ice-cold air over me. "He might not be here too. If he was foolish enough to come here on his merit, then there are fates worse than death and you'll do well to remember that little human."

"Whatever." I puffed out an ice-laden breath. Surely, he'd understand everything happening in his kingdom, but then again, the Fae King hadn't known about the Trappers until it was too late to stop their massacre.

"Ye, Gods, human, do you have a death wish?"

"You've all but told me I'll be dead before Roisin returns, so get on with killing me."

He laughed. "You believe I brought you outside to kill you?"

I nodded but held my ground.

He snorted. "I'd send my guards to dispose of you if that was my intention. I wouldn't waste my time on such puny matters."

"Except Roisin will be upset if you order me killed."

"Will she?"

"Yes," I said, knowing we'd shared more than a moment of giving in to our desires.

"She's a Fae Princess. She'll get over you when she finds her fated mate."

I hauled in a deep breath and held it. These people and their fated mates were driving me insane.

"Do demons have fated mates?"

"Yes."

"So where is yours?"

His fist struck my face so fast, I didn't see it coming, but the spurt of blood exploding from my nose and dribbling on my chin told me what had happened. The claret sprayed across the ice at my feet, painting the snow in an eerie tale of violence.

"No more questions about things that don't concern you." He stomped across the snowy path and out of the castle garden.

I touched a tentative finger to my nose and winced. Yep, broken. The bastard had broken my bones for asking him where his fated mate was. I guess it was a touchy subject and one I wouldn't ask again unless I was looking for another beating.

We walked silently across a field toward a group of horned demons sword fighting. My limbs itched to get in the fray with them and show them I wasn't a completely fragile human. That I had skills, and I'd hold my own. We stopped at the edge of the circle of demons, watching a pair in battle. My gaze skittered around all the different demons. One had pointed white horns pointing straight into the air from a flock of white hair. Another's skin was tinged red and his eyes glowed amber. The next demon appeared entirely human until his tongue flicked out of his mouth like a snake with a forked tongue.

"I made you," the Demon King said.

"Huh?" I blundered, awe-struck with the way the demons were fighting.

"The Fellowship of the Infinite Spring. You're my creation. My way to protect the Fae."

"Why?" I turned from the spectacular sight in front of me because this was more important.

"Because of family."

The swords clanged beside us, demons cheered, while others groaned as though they'd placed bets on who would win and who would lose. I couldn't take my eyes off the Demon King's face, though, because what he said made me believe Roisin was related to him. Which meant I was in love with a part Fae, part Siren, part Rage Demon.

"Well," I said, "You didn't do a very good job, did you?"

A collective sudden silence happened. A second later, they tossed me into the center of the fighting circle, thrust a sword into my hand, and a tall demon with long curled blue horns protruding from his head stood opposite me with a matching sword.

Well, shit, I had to open my big mouth again. There was nothing left for me to do than fight the demon opposite me. If I won, then I'd live to see Roisin again.

CHAPTER EIGHTEEN

ROISIN

"**B**RANDON WAS WITH ME," I said.

"And now?" Alister asked.

I pointed at the bookshelf. Everyone turned and squinted at the magical shelf as though Brandon would magically appear the way I had.

"The shelf is or was a magical portal." I studied the books on the shelf. Each title differed from the ones on the shelf when we'd left, but that was what the Fellowship said would happen when they removed a book from the shelves. "I took a book from the shelf."

Lorcan and Aislinn frowned at me.

Alister frowned even harder.

"There was a word hidden in the title and it seemed like a clue, but I didn't expect to be pulled into the Winter Court. Brandon tried saving me, but the magic pulled him through with me." I grabbed the old man's hand. "He protected me. Brandon said to say how much he loves you and his mother."

"He's dead?"

"No." I shook my head wildly, sending my long hair flying around my face. "He was very much alive when I left."

"But he doesn't believe he will be for long?"

"I'm sorry, I didn't want to leave him, but he told me to go, and then return for him. I intend to do that, but first, I need to speak with the Fae King and Queen."

All my family. I needed to talk to all of them. This affected them all if what the demon said was true. Did I believe the Demon King and his sister?

"Lorcan," I said, dropping Alister's hand and focusing on him. "Can you get all the family to the Summer Court?"

"What's going on?"

"I'll tell you at home. How long was I absent for?"

"Not long. Ciara and Sir Axis fixed the Spring of Life, and then I brought him back here. Aislinn noticed you weren't outside, so we came in here looking for you."

I rubbed a finger between my brows. "We were in the Winter Court a lot longer."

"Time would move differently there, as it does in the Summer Court," Lorcan said.

"I suspected as much."

That would mean the time would move a lot faster for Brandon in the Winter Court. He might be there for days while here, it was only minutes. I needed to hurry because what would the demons do to him in my absence? Surely, they wouldn't harm him when they wanted me to return to their realm.

"Is the Veil passable?" I asked.

"It is still locked, but the magic is no longer volatile. Sir Axis said it would become unstable again and so would the spring if we don't convince Father to unlock the Veil," Lorcan said.

"Aislinn, can you and Fallon come with me to the Summer Court while Lorcan and Pepper contact the rest of the family?"

Aislinn slid a dagger from the holster at her hip and twirled it around her fingers.

"Aye, are the demons a threat?"

"No." I turned and hurried toward the stairs. Every second away from Brandon felt like it mattered.

"Then what's the hurry?" she asked, catching up to me.

"I left Brandon there," I lowered my voice.

"Brandon? Oh, you mean the Fellowship member. I'm sure he's trained."

"Aye, but he almost froze to death in the Winter Court," I whispered.

"Ah, humans and their frailty."

We reached the top of the stairs from the underground library and burst into the open expanse of the secluded garden.

"Hurry," I said.

Aislinn called on the magic of the Veil. It snapped into place with ease in a swirling, magical, purple mist. My sibling's powers astounded me, but the same elemental magic steeped in my powers, only blinding white, like ice. I stepped into the Veil, not waiting a moment longer.

Aislinn and Fallon joined me then I waved a hand to Lorcan, knowing he'd bring the others home. There they would all learn what I had and together as a family we'd decide if it was true.

The Veil snapped shut, closing off the view of Earth and a sense of calm descended upon me. My first trip through the Veil hadn't felt this way. The magic had pulsed against me and made my powers erratic, now though everything vibrated right while shifting through the Veil as though the magic welcomed us.

"Ciara fixed it," Aislinn said.

"I realized she would."

Aislinn slid her dagger back into the holster and I hadn't even noticed she was still holding it, but then again, she was always holding her daggers. They seemed to comfort her when none of us had over the years. At least until Fallon. He slid an arm around her shoulders and pulled her to his side. She snuggled close to him as though a magnetic force pulled them together. Fated mates were such a beautiful sight to see. It was no wonder we all hungered for our own. No wonder I wanted to wait for mine, except now there was Brandon and the feelings I'd developed for him. The feelings he'd developed for me. Perhaps I should talk to Briana as she'd chosen a mate. She'd fallen in love knowing he wasn't the man destined for her. They'd been happy too until he'd died, but she was happier still now she was with her fated mate.

It was all so confusing, and I needed to keep my mind straight for the family's sake and not worry about myself.

The Veil parted near the tower Father had built away from everyone, hoping to keep track of all the Fae who left. He wanted to protect everyone since his father had failed to protect them against the Trappers.

Guards and a scribe surrounded the tower and jolted in surprise when they saw us open the Veil outside the tower.

"Princess Aislinn, Fallon. Princess Roisin?" the scribe said, glancing down at his parchment. "I don't have you on the list of travelers out of the kingdom." He looked back up. "We didn't realize you weren't safe."

"I was safe," I assured him.

"But you didn't take guards with you." He tapped his finger on the parchment. "The King put these things in place for a reason."

"Enough," I snapped. "I don't have time for this."

I strode off before he uttered another word. Aislinn and Fallon followed me, and soon their strides matched mine.

"He's right," Aislinn said. "Father will be upset to learn you were on Earth without guards. Let alone on Earth at all."

"The Fellowship are our guards. I was safe on Earth and in the Winter Court because I had Brandon with me."

Aislinn's gaze narrowed. "You keep mentioning the human's name."

"So?"

"Do you like him?"

"I..." I closed my mouth. What did I feel for him? Desire certainly. Like? It was more than like, but I said, "Aye."

"A human?" Aislinn nudged me in the ribs with her elbow. "What will Mother and Father say?"

"They can say what they like. I comprehend I can't... *like* him... he's not my fated mate."

Aislinn laughed. "Like? Oh, little Roisin."

"Stop it."

"Stop what?"

"Calling me young, or little. I'm tired of everyone treating me like a child. I'm a grown woman."

Aislinn placed a hand on my elbow and stopped walking, urging me to stop with her. I turned and faced her. She placed both hands on my shoulders and stared me in the eyes.

"You are, aren't you?"

She drew me into a hug and whispered, "I'm sorry I didn't notice sooner."

I wrapped my arms around her and hugged her back.

Aislinn sniffed. "I'm also sorry I was in such a bad mood all your life. From now on, I promise to be a better big sister."

My arms squeezed her harder. "I love you."

"I love you, too."

We hugged for a long time, both of us soaking up the moment of a new future where our relationship had changed for the better.

In the distance, the sound of galloping hooves echoed across the fields.

"Are they unicorns?" Fallon asked, awe-tinging his voice.

"Aye," Aislinn and I said in unison.

We both pulled apart and dabbed the tears in our eyes.

"If you like, I might coax one into coming closer."

Fallon's eyes bulged. "Ah, no thanks, they look dangerous."

I giggled. Fallon was a huge, muscular man who had fought in underground fights and won all of them. The idea of him being wary of unicorns was ridiculous.

"Are you scared of unicorns?" I teased.

"No, I just wanted to make you laugh." He flung an arm around both of our shoulders. "I grew up with horses and was around them all my life. One day, I'll take you up on the offer to get closer to the unicorns."

I was thankful my sister had found her fated mate, and he was a good match for her, would do anything for her, even make her sister laugh when the moment was emotional and needed lightning.

"See," I said. "Fated mates are worth waiting for."

"They are," Fallon agreed and kissed the top of Aislinn's head.

Up ahead, the palace appeared. The magical structure glistened under the Summer Court sun. It had always been spectacular to look at, but now it was as though extra magic was pulsing from the structure and the spring inside.

"I never noticed," Aislinn mumbled. "Not until now."

"What?" I asked.

"How depleted our powers were becoming."

"It was the same on Earth," Fallon said. "There was a sense something was wrong, but it's not until now that we healed the spring that I noticed the difference."

"Imagine what it'll be like when we heal Earth, too," I said.

Aislinn and Fallon stared at me for a second in agreement that the time had come for us to fix everything wrong between the two realms. Then we hurried toward the palace doors, to the home we'd always known, the one place where our powers made us immortal, and now we'd forever be immortal once we convinced Father to unlock the Veil.

Then I'd ask him and Mother about the truth of the demon's claim we were related to them.

CHAPTER NINETEEN
BRANDON

THE SWORD SWUNG AT my head. I ducked and rolled just in time to avoid the killing blow but tangled in the cape. I rolled again, flung the cape free from my body, and jumped to my feet. The demon stomped across the icy field sending up white shards of snow from his enormous feet. The determined step signaled he was intent on ending me. A gleam of death shone in his dark eyes. If I was under any illusion this wasn't a life or death situation, then his deadly glare told me the truth. His horns, an even darker black, looked even more deadly, but I suspected this was a sword fight only. Thank the Demon King if that was true, because my physical strength didn't match the demon by a long shot. He was well over seven feet tall, as were all of them. I was not a shrinking violet, but their supernatural strength was entirely different.

I bounced on the balls of my feet, taunting the demon closer until he came, took my bait, and stepped into the line of my swing. My muscle memory let go at once, swinging the sword toward the demon's chest, but he was too fast and had his sword up, blocking my blow. The sword vibrated up my entire arm with the strength of it.

My training kept me in good stead as I refused to show how hard the blow was. I dodged to the right, avoiding his quick return swing. It barely missed the crowd of circled demons. The ones it missed hurled insults and spat in his direction. Any other time and I would have laughed, but my head was on the line here.

If I won, they might show me a bit of respect instead of looking at me like the crap beneath their feet.

We circled each other until the demons yelled in frustration for us to get on with it. Luckily for me, it broke the demon's composure, and he raced forward. While he was quick, he wasn't as agile as me. I held my ground as the tip of his sword blade aimed for my head. At the last second, I ducked and swung my sword into the side of his ribs. The blade hit with precision, sliding into the demon's flesh with ease considering his hulking mass. Were the blades made from special metal?

The demon grunted, slammed a hand over the wound in his side and cursed. Blood gushed freely between his fingers. He stepped back, the flesh parting to reveal the glistening white bone beneath. The blow had been deeper than I realized. Than the demon realized. He staggered and fell to his knees, dropping his sword on the icy ground as though admitting defeat.

Well, shit, now what?

The crowd of demons was silent as they stared at their fallen comrade. Had I made a grave mistake? Would they all turn on me now? As though they'd read my mind, their gazes lifted and focused on me. Ice-cold dread coursed through my body, and it had nothing to do with the cold of the snow.

Ice crunched under boots to my left, but I didn't dare take my eyes off the demons staring at me.

"Congratulations," the Demon King said. "You won."

I finally chanced a glance at Rexan, but I knew better than to call him that out here. He lifted my hand, holding the sword up high.

"Victor," he yelled.

The crowd of demons yelled too, and then one by one, wings flared from their backs, and they took flight into the sky. All apart from the felled demon.

The Demon King dropped my hand and stepped back. "I have things to attend to. Kal, take Brandon with you to the infirmary."

"Wait, what do I need the infirmary for?"

"They'll fix your broken nose."

Right, I'd forgotten about the punch to my face from the Demon King, but I'd had worse blows during training for the Fellowship.

"I'm glad the Fellowship training is still accurate," he said. "Humans these days rely on guns and bullets."

"We've added those to our training, too."

"Human-made weapons won't kill us."

"They might slow you down."

"Perhaps." He inclined his head and with a flare of his leathery wings, he launched into the sky.

His form disappeared in no time at all, his wings were that large and powerful.

Kal clambered to his feet and walked toward me. The blood was still gushing from his wound, over his fingers, and dripping on the snow in red splotches. I shivered now the adrenaline of the fight had worn off.

"Come," Kal grunted and stomped through the snowy area back toward the castle.

I followed behind him, still holding the sword. Spotting the cape, I stooped and picked it up, wrapped it around my shoulders again, grateful for the added layer of warmth and protection from the elements of the Winter Court. The King was right. I'd freeze to death out here before I ever found a way out of the realm, and the only building I saw was the massive castle I'd come from.

As we walked toward the castle, Kal took a path to the left and led us around the building. I guess I was wrong. In front of me was a small hut, smoke billowing out of a chimney. The cottage with the thatched room reminded me of our old house back home in Ireland, the one we lived in with Grandfather. A sudden pang of homesickness jolted my chest. The demon glanced behind him as though he'd sensed my emotion, but that wasn't possible, was it?

The path to the cottage was well kept, as though someone was outside every hour sweeping the snow from the cobblestones, which was a strange thought as the rest of the kingdom appeared to revel in the continuous coverage of the white snowflakes.

Kal knocked on the door and it creaked inward as though the hinges needed a good oiling. I followed him inside the small cottage surprised the infirmary was so cramped, but then again, demons were immortal, so wouldn't they heal themselves, so why did they need an infirmary to begin with?

"Hey, old man," Kal said. "See to my wound."

A gray-haired man hobbled forward on a cane. "Who'd you piss off this time, Kal?"

"Some tiny human." He hooked a thumb in my direction.

The old man lifted his weathered face and stared at me. It was like I was looking at Grandfather, but with another fifty years added to his face. Time hadn't been kind to whoever this was. Wrinkle lines creased his face that would rival the worst material in history. His mouth fell open, revealing a toothless cavern.

"I'm sorry." He snapped his mouth shut and wobbled over to me. "You look..."

His hand lifted, and I took a step backward, hitting the door. I reached for the doorknob. The maniacal gleam in his eyes set all my senses alert.

"Wait, don't leave." He snagged my arm with his gnarled hands. "It's like looking in a mirror."

"You're crazy." I shook my head and arm, but the man was strong considering he was so old.

"Ye, Gods, you even sound like I did at that age." He laughed. "I never thought I'd see you." Tears welled in his eyes. "It is you, isn't it?"

"Whoever you think I am..."

"Brandon." He gulped. "My son."

CHAPTER TWENTY
ROISIN

G RIER, FATHER'S AIDE, OPENED the palace doors as though he was expecting us to arrive, but then he'd always done so.

"Welcome home." He bobbed.

"Grier, can you fetch Father and Mother, please?"

"Certainly, they're walking in the rose garden."

"Father is well?" I asked.

"Better than ever." Grier smiled.

"Never mind, we'll find them."

I raced through the palace, eager to find my father. When I'd left, he'd been lying in bed about to die. We'd all never imagined we'd lose our immortality, and die, but Father had put his own life on the line to keep the rest of the Fae alive. Sir Axis fixing the spring had healed everything. Well, almost everything according to Sir Axis, and since he'd helped us, I believed him when he said the spring would languish again if Father didn't unlock the Veil.

Aislinn and Fallon ran behind me. Our footfalls were loud through the marble hallways as though they were the pounding of our hearts. We burst through the glass doors on the patio and into the rose gardens. In the distance, I spotted them. My parents. The King and Queen held hands as they walked through the perfumed petals. I'd spent a lot of time in this garden painting the roses, so I recognized which way to run the fastest to get to them.

My feet barely touched the rich soil that now surged with power. Mother and Father stopped walking and turned to us. The radiant glow of the smile on her face made my happiness even brighter. Dia, I loved my mother so much. How would I tell her what the demons said?

Father opened his arms, and I launched myself into them.

"My baby girl," he mumbled while stroking my back in a soothing caress. "I'm all right. Everything will be all right now."

I couldn't stop the sudden onslaught of tears flowing from my eyes. They streamed down my face. Father had almost died. I'd kept my belief that Ciara would find a cure and because of that, I'd never given up hope. Despite that, the image of Father in bed fading away wouldn't leave my mind. I cried and cried until Mother's soothing voice started singing. Instantly my tears stopped, and I eased myself out of Father's arms.

"It's true." I stared at Mother.

"What's true, sweetheart?" Father asked.

I shook my head and dashed the tears from my cheeks, dropping my gaze from Mother's face because I'd glimpsed worry in her eyes.

"Sir Axis fixed the spring," I said, because every member of our family needed to be here when I asked Mother for the truth. I was afraid the demon's words were all true.

"He did," Father said. "I owe him a great gratitude."

"You owe him unlocking the Veil."

"Roisin." He sighed.

"No, Father. It's time." I glanced at Mother. Saltine had sent her those words that it was almost time. Now I understood what she meant by them. "We need to talk as a family. Lorcan is fetching everyone as we speak."

"Agreed," Father said. "I've made decisions that have affected everyone, but I can't say I'm sorry about them because they kept you all safe for many years."

"Father," Aislinn said before stepping forward and embracing him. "I'm happy to see you well."

Father returned her embrace and eyed Fallon over her shoulder.

Aislinn stepped back and pulled Fallon forward. "This is my fated mate, Fallon."

They nodded at each other.

"Your mother told me you'd mated," Father said. "I'm happy for you both."

Mother cleared her throat. "Let's head into the dining hall."

"It's not dinnertime," Aislinn said.

"No, but we'll need a large table if everyone is coming home with their mate," Mother said. "It makes me so happy to learn you've found them."

All except me.

Her gaze landed on me. "You'll find yours when the time is right."

"I understand that, Mother." I turned and walked back inside the palace. She knew. The words pounded inside my head. She'd hidden it from us for years that we were part Siren, part Rage Demon.

Anger welled deep in my stomach. Why wouldn't she tell us about our heritage? We'd lost all our family members to the Trappers, but we had more we didn't even know about. It would have been better to understand we had more family. Better to ease the loss the others had experienced, and for me. I would have grown up knowing family instead of believing there was only us. I didn't have time for this anger, though. Not when I needed to get back to the Winter Court and save Brandon. The longer I was away from him, the more the need to return to him grew. I couldn't have fallen in love with him, could I?

I paced to the dining hall and kept my pacing inside the room. Aislinn and Fallon sat at the table. Father stopped my pacing for a second, cupped my cheek in his hand, nodded his head, and let me go back to pacing. He understood me too well to realize I would settle right now. My fingers itched to throw paint on a canvas, to let the emotions out creatively. I paused at the end of the room and stared at the rose painting hanging on the wall. It was one of mine, as were all the paintings in the palace. They were all so pretty. My thoughts turned to the one I'd painted of Brandon, and so did his teasing words about painting him naked. I'd very much like to do that. Then I'd hang the painting in my bed chambers where I'd stare at Brandon any time I wanted.

Mother stood at the window and stared outside. Father stood by her side, his hand on her lower back, offering her his unwavering support as always. Did he know too?

Why was I so angry with them?

The door opened and Saoirse and Arrow walked into the room with their baby. Ailbhe. Behind them were Briana and Sledge. Saoirse and Briana took one look at Father and rushed across the room. He hugged them both at the same time.

"My girls," he muttered. "You both look well. I see your fated mates are treating you well on Earth."

"He is," they said in unison.

"Let me see my grandchild." Father held out his arms.

Arrow stepped forward and handed Father the baby. Ailbhe gurgled as though trying to talk. Father smiled.

"I thought I wouldn't see you grow up into the powerful man you'll become," Father said.

Ailbhe gurgled back.

"If only Sophia was here to translate for me," Father said.

As if summoned by her name, Sophia walked through the door with Rian, Lorcan, and Pepper. Rian strode toward Father, and they embraced in a back-thumping display of manly affection. Lorcan hung back, his chin low, and knowing my brother as I did, I recognized he was struggling with his emotions.

"You are well on Earth too?" Father asked.

"Aye, Father," Rian said. "I experienced the healing of the spring as soon as it happened."

"That is good news." He turned to Sophia. "And Earth?"

"The vibrations are still out of sync."

Father's lips firmed. "I was afraid of that."

Ailbhe gurgled again.

"What did he say?" Father asked Sophia since she was a jaguar shifter and understood shifters' young as Ailbhe was part wolf shifter.

Sophia smiled. "He's hungry."

Everyone laughed.

"Food will be along shortly," Mother said.

"I hope you would not eat without us," Ciara said, walking into the dining hall and holding hands with Malachi.

"Us?" Mother asked.

"Aye, Malachi is my fated mate, and we've marked each other."

I rushed over and hugged her before anyone else. She squeezed me back and then moved on to hugging the rest of the family one at a time until she reached Father. He dragged her in for a deep embrace.

"I'm happy for you both." He kissed the top of her head and released her. Then he glanced around the room at all his children. All his mated children except me. His youngest child he still called a baby girl. What would he say if I said I'd developed feelings for a human?

Mother embraced Ciara, then Malachi. "You've always been a part of the family."

"Thank you," Malachi said.

He'd been Ciara's best friend since they were born on the same day they'd grown up side by side, always together. Fate had been a part of their lives for longer than any of us had realized.

"Fate works in strange ways," I said.

Servers entered the room and placed platters of food on the table. Everyone claimed a seat and chatted happily as though they'd forgotten I'd asked them to come here. I didn't want to ruin the happy family moment. The togetherness. Love poured throughout the room.

Father placed his hand over mine. "What is it, Roisin?"

Drawing in a steadying breath, I pushed back my chair and stood.

"I asked you all to come here today because I was told something that affects us all." My gaze found Mother.

She gulped and pushed back her chair. "Roisin, don't."

"Don't what, Mother?"

She kept her stare on the stubborn tilt of my face and recognized I would tell her secrets.

A deep sigh escaped before she said, "Let me talk first."

I nodded and returned to my seat.

"A long time ago, I made a deal with Saltine," Mother said. "And now it's time for me to reveal what that deal was."

CHAPTER TWENTY-ONE
BRANDON

"**S**AY WHAT NOW?" I blabbered.

How was this old man my father? He wouldn't be this old. He couldn't be this old. This man was older than my grandfather, I was sure of that.

The doorknob pressed into my hand. The need to escape was even more overwhelming. Were the demons trying to trick me? I wouldn't put it past them.

"My father left me when I was a baby. You're too old to be him."

The old man touched his wrinkled face. "This realm isn't kind to humans. It ages us faster than Earth."

"No way. I don't believe you. The demons put you up to this, didn't they?"

"I made a deal with the Demon King."

"What deal?"

Curiosity kept me inside the cottage even though I still wanted to leave.

The old man heaved a sigh as though the very thought of the deal caused him great agony. "I can't reveal the details of the deal to anyone otherwise it becomes void."

"Handy," I scoffed.

"Brandon, listen to me," he implored.

"No. If you are my father, then why would I listen to you when you abandoned me?"

"I didn't want to. Trust me, I didn't want to leave you or your mother." His eyes glistened. "How is she?"

"None of your business."

"She's still alive though, isn't she?" He gripped my shoulders. "Tell me she's still alive."

The desperation in his voice cracked the resolve in me. Even if I didn't believe we were talking about the same person, I still said, "Yes, she's still alive."

His grip slackened. "Good. Good."

Kal groaned dramatically and slumped onto the floor.

"Shit," the old man said. "I have to tend to him. You cut him with that sword you're carrying?"

"Yes."

The old man hurried to the shelves along the side of the wall drew a jar down, popped the lid, and pulled out a dried leaf. He placed it in a mortar and pestle, added a drop of liquid from a silver jug, and ground them together. I watched, fascinated by his movements. They reminded me so much of Grandfather and if I was honest, my own. He crouched next to the fallen demon who was still holding his injured side. The old man wrenched his hand away and then slapped the paste on the wound. It sizzled as though it was a piece of meat cooking and mustard yellow smoke rose into the air.

"Open the door. Quickly. And stand out of the way."

I stared at the old man still trying to believe what he'd said and not believe it at the same time.

"You have three seconds. Hurry."

I flung the door open just as the demon sat up straight, Kal lurched to his feet and ran for the door. As soon as he was outside, he launched into the closest pile of snow and rolled around until the sizzling and smoking of his flesh stopped. I stepped onto the porch and watched in fascinated horror as the demon stood, dusting off the snow as though dusting lint off an expensive suit.

"Thanks, old man." Kal saluted, then walked off into the snowy fields beyond the cottage.

"What just happened?" I turned around to the old man still standing in the cottage's warmth.

"Come in and close the door and I'll tell you."

My gaze flickered to the castle where they'd locked me in a room, to the open white fields that promised me only freezing to death, to the interior of the warm cottage where neither imprisonment nor death awaited me. I stepped inside and shut the door, but looking at the old man, if this was my father, then my fate was worse than death. If I was stuck in the Winter Court, I'd age like him.

He gave a wracking cough then threw another log on the fire sending red sparks into the air.

"Demon iron hurts demons. I never understood why they train with it." He shook his head.

I lifted the sword and studied the blade under the glowing firelight and the few lit candles inside the cottage. I'd assumed the sword was different but knowing they'd left me with a sword that injured them made little sense.

"Why would the Demon King leave me with a sword that can injure them?" I asked aloud because I needed answers.

"My guess is so you're not an easy target. Demons don't take kindly to humans."

"I noticed."

"Keep it close to you."

"A scabbard would be good."

The old man held up his finger and then shuffled over to a cupboard. He opened the door and muttered under his breath.

"Aha!" He shuffled back holding a long leather strip in his hand. "I thought I had one in here."

"Thanks." I took the leather and strapped it to my body then placed the sword in the holster.

"You won't be able to kill a demon with that though, so don't be getting any fancy ideas in your head."

I snorted. "I won't."

But maybe, just maybe I'd persuade a demon to portal me out of the Winter Court and back home, or better yet, to wherever Roisin was.

"So, son, how did you get here? Did you make a deal with a demon?"

"I'm not your son."

The old man opened his mouth, and I held up my finger.

"I came through a magical bookshelf. I'd never make a deal with a demon."

The old man grew whiter still, the wrinkles on his face even more pronounced.

"I... no... you couldn't have."

"I assure you I did."

"But humans can't pass through the bookshelf. The King didn't design it that way." He lowered his eyes and sat heavily in a chair. "You can't be my son then."

"I'm human."

"Not possible." He lifted his gaze.

I shrugged. "I came through with a Fae Princess."

His shoulders straightened. "A Fae Princess is in the Winter Court?"

"Not anymore."

He sagged again.

"Okay, old man, are you going to tell me what's going on?"

He pointed at the seat opposite him. I walked over to it, removed the cloak because I was getting hot in the cottage, and sat on the chair.

"The magical bookshelf in the Fellowship connects to the Winter Court. The Demon King created it to remove the knowledge of certain things from ever coming to light."

"What things?"

"I'm not one hundred percent sure. There are rumors and speculation, but only the Demon King knows the truth. He was the one who made it."

Was it to do with Roisin's family being connected to the demons? Was that the knowledge the Demon King was gatekeeping?

The old man reached a shaky hand for a mug on the nearby table, the contents spilled onto his clothes as he brought it to his mouth.

After taking a sip, he said, "The Demon King created the Fellowship."

"He told me that already."

His hand shook even more. "He'll never let you leave now. Just like me."

"There's no chance in hell I'm staying here."

He slammed the mug onto the table spilling even more liquid. "There's no escaping the Winter Court. Not for you. Not for me."

I leaned forward. "How long have you been here?"

"You should know more than me." He leaned forward too. "You were just a baby. How old are you now?"

I shook my head. "I can't be your son."

"Can't you?"

The door burst open sending in a gust of icy air. Tay stood in the doorway and placed her hands on her hips.

"Now what is my brother up to?" She snapped her fingers. "Come, human, time to return to the castle."

"I'm not a dog you can call to heel," I said.

Her eyes landed on the sword at my side. "So, what, you plan to fight me? Then what will happen to your precious princess when she returns for you?"

"You wouldn't hurt Roisin."

Her dark eyes narrowed. "Don't test me. Come now or I'll leave you outside."

"Go, son," the old man pleaded. "You'll never survive the cold of this place." He shuddered as though cold and scared.

I stood and donned the cape. I didn't care if I died outside, but if they'd hurt Roisin, then I needed to be alive to protect her. Everything in me said the only way to die was to protect the Fae Princess I'd fallen in love with.

CHAPTER TWENTY-TWO

ROISIN

MOTHER DROPPED HER GAZE to Father. "Forgive me, please?"

"I love you, Niamh. There's nothing you can do that would change my feelings for you."

"But I've kept a secret from you for years."

Father's eyes widened. "Why?"

"Your grandfather died at the hands of a Siren."

"What does my grandfather's death have to do with your secret?"

"Everyone comprehended your father despised the Sirens because of it," Mother said.

"The same way we despised the Trappers."

"But we only despised the ones who hurt us, not all humans," Mother said. "Your father seemed to blame them all."

"He believed it was the Siren Queen herself who killed him. It wasn't until later we learned it was her evil twin sister. By then, he'd found it hard to not despise them."

"Every Fae understood not to mention Sirens to your father when he was the king," Mother said. "When he requested I sing at your two hundredth birthday ball, I didn't understand where my unusual power came from. It wasn't until Saltine..."

"You'd believed your voice had tricked me into thinking I was your mate," Father said.

"Aye."

"But I recognized you were mine, and it wasn't a trick of magic."

"You did." Mother's eyes welled with tears. "I wanted to believe you, to believe I was yours. It wasn't until Saltine did her spell that I realized for sure my power hadn't tricked you."

"I remember taking you to Saltine's house, but you never said what happened, and it wasn't in your memories when I marked you."

"She'd placed a blocking spell on that moment so you wouldn't see. She thought you wouldn't want me if you learned the truth."

"I always want you."

Mother sucked in a deep breath, then said, "Saltine's spell revealed I had Siren blood in my veins and that was the reason my voice tricked men into thinking they were my mate."

Father stood slowly.

Mother rushed on to say, "She did a spell to remove the power of the Sirens and made it so I wouldn't inadvertently pass it on to any of my children as had happened on the rare occasion in my family. It was such an unusual power, and it didn't happen often. No one understood where it came from. There were rumors, of course, but we didn't believe them. Siren offspring always stay in the Autumn Court and become Sirens, so we didn't think it was real."

"But it was real?" Father asked.

Mother nodded and bit her lip. "Do you hate me?"

Father frowned. "Why would I hate you?"

"I lied to you for years. I'm a descendant of the people who killed your grandfather."

"Oh, Niamh, I'd never hate you. You could tell me a thousand lies, and I'd still love you. You could have been the one to kill my grandfather, and I'd still love you. My love for you is endless." He placed his hands on her shoulders. "There is nothing, absolutely nothing that would stop me from loving you."

Mother sniffed, then buried her face in Father's chest. He wrapped his arms around her and held her while she sobbed.

"I can't believe you kept the secret for so long." He brushed her hair back from her face. "Why?"

"Saltine said I needed to."

Father kissed her forehead.

"So that means we all have Siren blood in us?" Aislinn asked.

"Aye," Mother said.

A ripple of murmurs ran through everyone, but I stared at Mother and Father. The absolute love and devotion of fated mates had made me want to keep the rest to myself, but I had to consider Brandon, who'd sacrificed himself to help me.

"There's more," I said, standing once again. "Do you know, Mother?"

"Know what, sweetheart?"

I tilted my head to the side. "You don't know, do you?"

"I've told all my secrets."

I hauled in a breath. "While Father was unconscious, I went to Earth."

Father let go of Mother and opened his mouth.

"That's not all. I went to the Winter Court."

His mouth snapped shut.

"The Demon King told me we're related to Sirens. I learned your secret, Mother, but I didn't believe him. You know what else he told me?" I looked around at my siblings, then settled my gaze on Mother's face, so I'd be sure she didn't know this secret. "That we're also related to him!"

The shock on Mother's face wasn't fake. She didn't know. Father's face was equally shocked.

"They're holding Brandon, a member of the Fellowship who was protecting me, hostage, so I'll return with the family. The Demon King wants to talk to Mother in particular, but he wants to meet the rest of us. The rest of his family."

"No," Rian said, standing too. "They're lying."

"Why would they tell me the truth about the Siren heritage and lie about the Demon part?" I asked.

"I'm not sure," Rian said. "They're planning something. Perhaps they were the ones who sent the Trappers after us."

"Stop. The Trappers came from a person drinking from the Infinite Spring. The power corrupted them," Ciara said. "It's why the Fellowship protects it."

"No, the Fellowship protects us," I said.

"The two springs connect so the same thing," she said.

And so, the bickering went on between my brothers, sisters, and their fated mates. Mother and Father huddled together whispering, but each time I tried to listen to their conversation, my sister or brother would drag me back into the argument.

"Enough," Father bellowed. "Sit."

Everyone startled and returned to their seat.

"Your Mother and I will go to the Winter Court with Roisin." He glared at me as though he wanted to yell at me for going. "Rian, you'll stay here until I return. As will the rest of you." He glared at each of my siblings. "No more arguing. Period."

"Father?" Saoirse asked.

"Aye?"

"If it's true, is it a good thing or a bad thing that we're related to the demon royalty?"

"Demons are very loyal to their families, so if it's true, no harm will come to us, to any of you from the demons."

"And if it's a trap to kill you?" Lorcan asked.

"Then you'll all be in the best place to protect you."

"What about the Veil?" Ciara asked. "Sir Axis was quite clear you needed to lift the lock."

"I'll need to lift the lock to travel to the Winter Court," Father said.

I lifted the stone from my hidden pocket in the dress. "The demon princess gave me this. She said it would transport us to the Winter Court."

Father placed his hand over the rock. "No. We'll go in our way. Then I'm certain I'll have a way to get you and your mother out safely."

I didn't like his words. Did that mean he'd put his life on the line yet again to put our safety first?

"And just when we thought everything was going our way," Briana said.

I glanced across the table at Briana, to the man sitting beside her who was her fated mate. Sledge, the Alpha wolf shifter, so different from the Fae Briana had chosen as a mate until his untimely death at the hands of the Trappers.

"Roisin, we'll head to the tower," Father said.

"Why?" Briana asked.

"I need to destroy it to unlock the Veil," Father said. He tucked Mother's arm through his and led her from the dining hall.

Everyone followed. I didn't expect them to stay behind. I sidled up next to Briana as we walked out of the palace.

"Can I talk to you alone, please?" I glanced at Sledge beside her.

"Of course." She squeezed Sledge's arm, and he dropped behind us a few paces. "Wolf shifters have good hearing. He'll hear you, anyway."

"I understand, but I didn't want to upset the happiness you two have together."

Briana smiled. "You saw Mother and Father today. There is nothing that can tear apart fated mates."

"I saw. That's why this is even harder," I said. "Were you truly happy with your chosen mate?"

Briana's smile fluttered. "I have a lot of happy memories with him. I loved him greatly."

"That's what everyone said to me when explaining why you were so sad all the time. Was it worth it though? To love him and lose him? Are the happy memories enough to warrant the pain?"

Briana's steps slowed and gave us more distance from the rest of the family.

"You've fallen in love with a man who's not your fated mate?"

"I believe so."

"Oh, Roisin." She sighed. "I wouldn't wish that pain on my greatest enemy, let alone my sister."

"So, I should ignore my feelings and wait for my fated mate?"

She grasped my hand and squeezed. "I can't decide that for you. Only your heart can tell you if it wants to take that leap into love knowing it will end. If I'd known I'd lose a mate and a child, then no, I doubt if I had the chance to rewrite history that I'd do it again. I loved them both so very much and the pain was so great. It still is some days. Thank Dia fate sent me Sledge to heal my pain, to show me there's still love after experiencing a loss so intense that I didn't comprehend how to function."

I sniffed back the sudden onslaught of tears threatening to fall.

"Roisin, I recognize you don't like us telling you that you're young, but compared to the rest of us, you are. Now they fixed the spring you have endless years to find your fated mate."

"I understand all this, but..."

"But your heart wants him?"

"Aye. I don't understand how it happened, but it does."

Briana puffed out a laugh. "I tried to reject Sledge for so long because I didn't believe my heart would take loving and losing again, but my heart had other ideas too. Sometimes the brain and heart war yet the heart always wins."

"I'm glad your heart won. I like Sledge."

"Dia, don't say that. He already has too big an ego."

I glanced over my shoulder at the hulking wolf shifter. He smirked at me.

Laughingly, I said, "I doubt his ego can get any bigger."

"I heard that," Sledge said.

"I wanted you to," I said over my shoulder.

"So, who is it?" Briana asked.

"Brandon the Fellowship member."

"A human."

Behind us, Sledge let out a low whistle.

"So, you going back to the Winter Court isn't purely for what the demons told you?"

"I can't leave him there. He's only stuck there because of me."

"Mother and Father aren't dumb. They'll see how you feel about him, and then what?"

I shrugged because I still wasn't sure what I was going to do about my feelings for the human.

"So long as I rescue him, then that's all that matters. I'll decide about the other predicament later."

"Humans don't have a lot of later. At least when I chose my mate, he was Fae, and I'd expected him to live forever like me. You'd be signing up to have your heart broken in no time at all."

My heart was already breaking being away from him, so hearing her say all my thoughts out loud didn't stop the way my heart raced at the idea we'd soon be back in the Winter Court, and I'd soon be near Brandon again. My skin buzzed with power so fiercely, it surprised me ice didn't cover my hands.

We caught up to the rest of the family as they stood outside the tower. Father had made the tower to create a contained doorway through the Veil, so he'd still protect Fae when they traveled to Earth. He'd even issued guards to travel with anyone who left. Some Fae had tried it and returned. My brothers and sisters had used it too. I wouldn't get the chance.

Father was about to unlock the Veil and change Fae history.

CHAPTER TWENTY-THREE

ROISIN

A T FATHER'S COMMAND, ALL the guards and the scribe rushed back from the tower. No one had witnessed Father create the tower. One day it had appeared, but Father was so powerful anything was possible in his kingdom.

He kissed Mother in a passionate display that had all of us looking the other way.

"Everyone ready?" Father asked.

"For what?" I asked.

"Power unlike any other you've experienced." He grinned.

Mother stepped back with us children. Father lifted his arms into the air, his hands glowed a silver iridescence as power flared from him. The silver floated in the air, up over the tower. It swirled around the tower in a vortex until we couldn't see the building through the thickness of its magic. Faster and faster the vortex churned, then Father clapped his hands and the misty magic flared outward in an explosion, blasting our hair back from our faces. Once the mist cleared, the tower was no longer there.

Shivers danced up my arms as though my power was responding to Father's.

His hands glowed even brighter, then he kneeled and shoved them into the soil. The entire ground glowed with his power. It raced across the soil, under our feet, and further still until I imagined his magic covered the entire Summer Court.

Father's head drooped between his shoulders as the power pulsed in waves like water rushing over the land. Then his head snapped up, he raised his hands into the sky, and his power shot upward in a blast that turned the sky silver. He clapped his hands again, and the same blast of power exploded in the sky, except this time, tiny silver particles fell like millions upon millions of fireflies dancing in the evening light. Once they hit the soil, they disappeared as though the very ground was soaking in the power.

"It is accomplished," Father said.

I dropped to my knees, as did my brothers and sisters. The surge of power coming from the soil, and all around me was too much. My hands glowed. Ice covered them. I counted as I breathed, trying to reign back the pulsing power eager to escape. Impatient to reach for the now open Veil.

One by one, Father walked over to us and helped us to our feet.

"I'd forgotten," Rian said. "How it felt with the Veil unlocked."

Aislinn shook her glowing hands, reached for one of her daggers, then twirled it around her fingers in a way that calmed her. Soon her hands stopped glowing.

I glanced over at Saoirse who'd claimed her baby from Arrow and was talking excitedly with them. She, too, would have experienced this power before Father locked the Veil. It was only me and Ciara who were experiencing it for the first time. Ciara walked over to me and hugged me.

"You did it this time," she whispered into my ear. "You're the one who convinced Father to open the Veil. I realized it would be you."

I smiled. "Have you ever sensed anything so wonderful?"

"It's almost as good as marking my fated mate." She released me and winked at Malachi.

Malachi turned a light shade of pink. They were so sweet together. I was glad they'd had each other all their lives, even if they didn't realize how important they were to each other until leaving the Summer Court. Perhaps if the locked Veil hadn't muted our powers, then they would have realized it sooner.

"Be safe, and come back soon," she said.

"I will."

"Roisin," Father called.

I turned around to the open Veil. Father had parted it in another dazzling display of his silvery power. I'd never seen the Veil so vibrant, so alive as in this moment. It was a thing of beauty that I'd remember this moment forever. I ran into the Veil next to Father and Mother, who was standing beside him. Neither of them said goodbye to the others, and I didn't either. We'd be back. I had to believe we fixed the spring and the Veil to see the future for how bright it would be now our powers and immortality weren't at stake. Now my siblings were mated and happy. Now they'd have more children for me to be an aunty. I'd be able to travel to Earth and visit Saoirse, Arrow, and Ailbhe any time I wanted. Especially with the strength of the power pulsing in my body.

The magic of the Veil vibrated against my skin. Father grinned as though he experienced it, too.

"This is glorious!" He threw his head back and lifted his hands. "I'd forgotten too."

Mother laughed and lifted her hands, her power joined with Father.

"Fintan," she said. "Never regret keeping us safe all these years."

His head dropped back down, and he kissed her upturned lips quickly.

Should I wait to have a love like theirs? Or would the feelings I'd developed for Brandon be enough for now? Briana's words hadn't lessened the pull I had for Brandon. I couldn't explain the way my heart thudded every time I thought about him or the way my skin tightened and tingled knowing I'd soon be near him again.

Father lowered his hands and parted the Veil. "The Winter Court."

We stepped from our magical curtain into the icy wonderland of the demon kingdom. A flock of demons descended from the sky, swords before them, ready to take us down.

"Lower your swords," Father said. "We're here under invitation from the Demon King."

"We have no orders of visitors arriving," one guard said.

"I should have used the stone Tay gave me," I said.

"What stone?" asked the guard.

I lifted the warm stone from my pocket and showed it to the guards.

"Tay said to use it to return here."

"If she gave you one of those, then you're meant to be here," the guard said. "But not those two. You can return to wherever you came from."

Father puffed out his chest. "I'm King Fintan of the Summer Court and I'll wait here until you speak to your King."

Murmurs ran through the guards, then one demon guard took flight.

"We'll wait for word from the King," a guard said. "So long as you try nothing."

Father rolled his eyes, reminding me of Briana.

"The King requested our presence. We're not here to harm anyone."

The guard lowered his sword but kept it in his hand, still not trusting us. I imagined Father's guards would be the same in the Summer Court now the Veil was open. Would demons be able to travel there? Or was it just Fae still? I couldn't very well ask Father in front of the demons.

We waited for what seemed like an eternity before the guard returned.

"It's true," he said. "They're guests here. The King is waiting for them."

"Shit, we better hurry then," the guard said. "It'd be faster if you could fly."

"Alas, we don't have wings like you," Father said.

The guards sheathed their swords and marched with us through the snow. It reminded me of when I'd arrived here with Brandon and how he'd almost died out here. I hoped they had him locked up safely inside the castle where it was warm. How I hungered to see him again. It seemed like months had passed, but it hadn't even been a day for me. How long would it have been for him? Would he still want to see me?

The trek was endless through the white expanse of snow.

"It's so different to the Summer Court," Mother said.

Father chuckled and wrapped an arm around her shoulders before dropping an affectionate kiss on the top of her head.

"Whatever happens here, remember, I love you."

"I love you, too, Fintan," Mother said.

Up ahead grew the shape of the castle. Smoke billowed from a chimney that I hoped was Brandon's room. Every urge in my body said to run, but common sense said the guards might not take too kindly to that, so I kept pace with everyone. As we reached the castle, a pair of guards opened the double front doors. The other guards halted and watched us walk inside.

They'd decorated the foyer in red from the carpet to the wall coverings, to the wooden furniture with a red hue in the carved wood. Two more guards stood at the foot of the stairs in the grand entrance.

"Where to now?" I asked.

"Someone will be along to escort you soon," one guard said.

Mother walked over to a painting hanging on the wall. I joined her and examined the picture of a man and woman wrapped in each other's arms.

"It's almost as good as your paintings," Mother said.

"Please," the demon voice I recognized as Tay scoffed. "It's way better than Roisin's painting."

"How would you know?" Mother asked. "And who are you?"

"The better question is who are you?" Tay asked.

"I'm Niamh, Queen of the Fae."

Tay stumbled down the last step, which was so unusual for her normal competence.

"Now tell me who you are," Mother said. "No one talks about my daughter's paintings like that."

"You may call me Tay," she said. "Roisin's painting is quite good, but I suspect she needs practice perfecting the male body. The one she painted of the human didn't quite capture all his assets, if you know what I mean."

I blushed so hard my face burned.

Mother stared at me, but I rushed over to Tay.

"Where is Brandon?"

"Upstairs in the bedroom where you left him." Tay smirked as she looked at my mother over my shoulder.

What must my parents be thinking? That I'd slept with the human, no doubt.

"The King is waiting for you all. Follow me."

"I did what you wanted. Now release Brandon."

Tay turned and strode back up the stairs. "All in good time, little rose."

I scowled at her back as I followed her up the stairs. If she was family, I didn't like her very much. She looked over her shoulder at me and winked.

Mother touched my elbow. "Did you and the human..."

"No. He was asleep in a chair when I painted him. It was nothing like she's insinuating."

"Come now," Tay said. "I recognize the sight of kiss-ravaged lips when I see them."

I wished I had one of Aislinn's daggers strapped to my body, so I'd stab her through the heart and shut her up for a minute. Instead, a pulse of my power flared from my hands and hit her back.

"I guess the ice princess has some bite to her after all."

"You'll find out how much if you don't bring me Brandon."

Tay held up her hands. "We have family matters to discuss first before you take the human back to Earth. I have no intention of keeping him here. He was simply a way to make sure you returned."

I opened my mouth to say more, but Mother placed a calming hand on my arm and hummed a soft tune. At once, the urge to cause Tay bodily harm diminished and peace swamped my mind. Saltine may have removed the luring call of a Siren from Mother's voice, but she'd left her with other powers in her voice. I hadn't even thought about where Mother's unusual powers came from. She was simply my mother, and I'd accepted who she was as a wonderful, caring parent.

What a sheltered life I'd lived staying in the Summer Court.

Well, no more. Now the Veil was open, I'd see everything possible. Starting with Brandon.

"If Roisin would like to see the Fellowship member to confirm he's still alive, then she shall do so before we talk to the King," Father said.

"Fine," Tay said.

We reached the top of the stairs and a guard rushed forward.

"Take Princess Roisin to the human."

The guard nodded. I cast a panicked glance at my parents, torn between separating from them and finding Brandon.

"Go," Father said.

Mother clutched his arm and watched me turn around. I hoped I hadn't made a great mistake by leaving them. I hoped Brandon was still alive, and this wasn't a ploy to kill my parents and I'd just sent them to the slaughter.

CHAPTER TWENTY-FOUR
BRANDON'

I COULDN'T SIT IN this opulent room any longer. It'd been weeks, maybe months, since Roisin had left. They'd taken me outside every day to fight with the demons, and I'd relished slicing them with their swords. They'd nicked me a few times. I hadn't ventured back to the old man's cottage again, even though they'd offered for me to go to the infirmary with my victims. A servant had delivered a jar of magical healing salve to my room, and I wasn't too stubborn to not use it, but I didn't want to listen to the old man's lies again. There was no way in hell he was my father. He was too old. It was as simple as that, I kept telling myself. Part of me didn't want to believe the man who'd abandoned his duties, his wife, and his son. The hurt from knowing my father had left me as a baby ran deep. Hadn't he wanted me enough to stay?

Yet the niggle in my mind made me think about him.

But I'd finally worked out who I'd try to coerce into taking me home. Every three meals, a smaller, female demon with dainty protrusions on her forehead would come to my room with a tray. She'd given me the once-over every time. It grossed me out because she wasn't Roisin. My heart beat for her now and other women were nonexistent.

My sword hand itched to threaten her. Every second away from Roisin, not knowing if she was safe was making it impossible to focus. I paced the room, trying to calm my emotions, but whenever I thought of Roisin, they always flared out of control. Time ticked past when I'd figured out the meals usually arrived.

Had they finally given up on keeping me alive?

A knock pounded on the door. It always amused me they announced their presence before opening the door.

The door swung in, and the object of my obsession stepped into the room.

"Roisin?" I asked stupidly because it was her.

"I said I'd be back for you," she said, lifting her chin.

The door closed behind us, and the lock clicked into place. There went my chance at escape, but I couldn't complain with Roisin in the same room as me again.

"That you did." I strode across the room and paused a bare centimeter before her.

Her breath hitched as though the closeness of our bodies affected her as much as me. The longer I stared, the wider the blue of her eyes grew until they swallowed me in the magical depths. Her tongue darted out to wet her lips.

"I missed you. How about a kiss hello?"

"I'm not sure that's appropriate." She tossed back her hair over her shoulders, leaving me the creamy expanse of her neck I'd dreamed about nuzzling.

I leaned forward, testing her resolve. "What about a little kiss here?"

She didn't move, so I lowered my lips to her neck. The second my lips touched her skin, I grasped I was done for. I wouldn't be able to stop unless she said the word no.

"That's acceptable." She shivered under my lips.

"What about here?" I kissed her lower along her collarbone.

"Dia." She moaned.

"Yes?"

"Yes!"

I slid my arms around her back and drew her body into the warmth of mine. How I hungered for her. Craved her like a drug. My lips kissed her tender neck over and over, testing which parts of kissing her made her shiver and moan the most.

"Will you kiss me now?" I asked before nibbling her jaw.

"Yes, Brandon, yes," she said throatily.

My lips claimed hers, slanting over them and devouring every inch she gave to me. Her tongue met mine in a hungry kiss that made my cock harder than it ever had been before. Every time she turned me on, it grew harder than I'd ever thought possible. We kissed so much she began rubbing her body against mine in need. I understood how she felt. How she hungered for more.

I backed toward the bed, easing her with me until the backs of my knees hit the mattress and then I tumbled backward, taking her on top of my body. She lifted her head and gasped, then giggled. Music to my ears. I brushed her long hair back from her face then held it in the palms of my hands like a precious flower, and she was, she was my Roisin.

"Roisin what happened?"

"Talk later." She smiled shyly. "I want you to do those things to me you promised."

"What things might those be?" I brushed a thumb over her bottom lip.

Her tongue darted out and licked the pad of my thumb. I groaned, imagining her tongue licking my cock. Her cheeks tinged a delicate pink hue. I loved seeing her blush.

I loved making her blush.

"Do we have hours?" I asked.

"They never said how long they'd give me. I was only supposed to see if you were still alive and safe." She touched the side of my face where an ugly bruise had formed from one fight. "What happened?"

"Training, that's all. Nothing bad."

"Nothing bad?" She sat up and looked at me.

I'd sustained a few injuries during the sword fighting sessions, but thankfully, no hits with the swords. They'd all been sneaky elbows or knees I hadn't anticipated quickly enough. The demons liked to fight dirty, and I was picking up their skills.

Roisin tugged my top up and hissed at the sight of my bruised ribs. Those were painful after a solid knee had doubled me over in pain. I'd scored a stab wound through the demon's thigh, though, so I'd won in the end.

"Is this not bad?" She poked my bruise, making me wince. "And you pulled me on top of you. What were you thinking?"

"I was thinking about kissing you, pleasuring you, if that wasn't obvious." I placed my hands behind my head and let her look her fill of my body. Her gaze darted everywhere as though she didn't know which part of me to look at. As though she loved the extra muscles I'd developed while fighting the demons.

She placed her hand on my bruised ribs gently this time. "How bad is it?"

"I've had worse during training back home." I placed my hand on top of hers, eager to keep her touching me.

"If we were in the Summer Court, I'd heal these with our Spring of Life."

"I didn't think humans could go to the Fae Kingdom."

"They can't." She shook her head as though to herself. "I still don't believe they can, but I can't be sure. Father unlocked the Veil."

"That's great news." I sat up, bringing our chests together and trapping her hand between us.

"It is. We'll fix everything once we sort out this business with the Demon King."

"You still don't believe him?" I rubbed my hands up and down her back, enjoying the way her body moved with the caress. "I didn't determine if they were lying to you."

"He might tell the truth."

"No shit?"

She giggled. "I'm not sure what that means, but it sounds funny."

"You feel good in my arms." I ran my finger along the top of her dress. "I want to have you naked against me."

Roisin blushed harder. "I'd like that too."

"Can I?" I tugged on her dress.

She nodded.

"Tell me what you want." The swell of her breasts peeking along the seam of her dress tempted me too much. I kissed the delicate skin.

"Touch me."

"I thought you'd never ask." My fingers tugged the top of her dress down and her breasts spilled free. Thank heavens she wasn't wearing a bra. Wait, did that mean she also wasn't wearing panties? My hands slid to her waist and searched for the telltale sign. Nope, no panties either. I'd died and gone to heaven, which explained my fantasy coming to life.

"I thought you were going to touch me?" She pouted.

"Right away, Princess." I snapped my hands up to her breasts and greedily cupped them both in the palms of my hands.

She bit her lip as she watched my hands fondle her breasts. I stroked my thumb over the hard peaks of her nipples, watching them with her as they tightened even further.

"I've never seen breasts as beautiful as yours."

"Have you seen a lot?" she asked.

"I'm not a virgin, Roisin." I paused what I was doing to stare at her face. Would she still want me, knowing I hadn't saved myself for fated love the way she was? But then, she was letting me touch her so maybe she'd changed her mind about waiting for her fated mate?

"I never thought you were." She leaned back and pulled her dress back up covering the best breasts I'd ever seen. I wanted to kiss them, suck them, and rub my cock against them until I came all over them and marked them as mine.

"Then why ask?"

She dropped her gaze to my cock, straining in my pants between us.

"Do you want to see me naked?"

"I don't have any other men to compare you to." Her tongue touched her lip.

"Anything you want, just ask, Roisin. I'll happily give it to you."

She glanced toward the door. "I'm not sure how long we have alone."

"So, a little show and tell is all we'll do right now, yeah?"

She nodded her head.

"Hop up, love, then you'll see me better."

My fingers flew to my pants. I'd never been this eager to show a woman my body before, but this was different. This was the woman I was in love with.

CHAPTER TWENTY-FIVE

ROISIN

WORDS COULDN'T DESCRIBE HOW excited I was to see Brandon naked. His fingers hovered at the waist of his pants until I climbed off his body. He leaned back on his elbows and slid his pants down. The tip of his cock peeked over the material, then part of the length, then the entire thing throbbed into view.

It was glorious.

Long and proud, reaching to his belly button. Muscles rippled on his stomach. His thighs were firm and muscular, too. Staring at him made everything below my waist clench with desire.

"Well?" Brandon asked.

"You're bigger than I imagined."

"Imagine my dick a lot, did you?"

My cheeks heated. I'd had little spare time to imagine his cock since I'd left him, but the thought had popped into my mind at least once. Especially after he'd promised to love me for hours.

I glanced at the door again. This was so wrong, yet it was so right, but what if a demon walked in?

"What's the scowl for?" He tugged his pants back up.

"We shouldn't do this. Forget it ever happened."

He fixed his clothes, jumped from the bed, and gathered me in his arms. "Not a chance in hell that I'll forget anything about you. About anything we do together. Let me make it very clear." He kissed my forehead. "I love you."

"You can't love me," I sobbed.

"I can and I do." He smiled. "You can't decide my feelings for you. Just as I can't decide yours for me. If you want me to back off, then I will."

"I'm so confused." My head lowered to his shoulder, and I rested it on the thick cord of muscles. "I've grown up my entire life thinking I'd find my fated mate and love him... then I met you."

"Does that mean you love me, too?"

"Perhaps I do."

His chest bounced under my head as he laughed. "I'll take that 'perhaps' for now until you're ready to say the words to me."

"What if I'm never ready?"

"Then I'll still love you."

My heart swelled even more for this man. He sounded so sure of his feelings for me, the same way my parents were sure of their feelings for each other. Could I deny my feelings for him? Could I ignore them and wait for who knows how long until my fated mate came along?

"Even when I'm old and gray and you're still this knockout beautiful immortal Fae Princess, I'll love you."

I lifted my head and stared into the devotion in his eyes. He meant every word he said. The unfairness that he wasn't my fated mate sunk my heart into the pit of my stomach. If I gave into the feelings I had for him, one day I'd break his heart in two by leaving him for another man. An immortal man who'd never die on me like Brandon would.

He claimed my lips in another kiss, and I clung to him like a desperate woman. And I was. Desperate to have him. Impatient for those hours of loving he'd promised me. Eager to have him forever.

A knock on the door had us skidding apart. I swiped a hand over my mouth, remembering what Tay had said about my lips looking kiss-ravaged. I didn't even have time to dash into the bathroom and check before the door swung open and Tay herself stood in the doorway.

"Sorry kids, time's up. My brother won't wait any longer for you two to get your rocks off."

"Don't insult the Princess," Brandon said, stepping toward a sword in the corner.

"Ah-ah. The sword stays there, hero." Tay waggled her finger at him. "Princess Roisin, your parents are waiting. You've seen Brandon is quite safe and sound."

"Aye," I said. "I'll come with you."

I couldn't stay in the room and ignore my responsibilities to my family. It was the reason I brought my parents here. So, they'd learn the truth from the Demon King.

"I'll be back," I said to Brandon. "As soon as this is over, I'll take you home."

Brandon nodded.

Tay walked out of the room, and I followed close behind her. She locked the door.

"Do you need to lock him in?"

"Safety first and always. You should comprehend that as a princess yourself."

"You injured him while he was here."

Tay shrugged. "He refuses to see the healer at the infirmary."

"Why?"

"You'd have to ask him that."

I intended to do so the moment I returned to him. First, there was the matter of this meeting with the Demon King and my parents. Tay led me into a formal sitting room. My parents sat on a two-seater couch holding hands. Opposite them sat the Demon King, lounging back in a single chair. Tay took the seat next to the Demon King. I sat in the chair nearest my parents.

"Is the Fellowship member safe?" Father asked.

"Aye, although he's injured from sword fighting, he said."

"There was no point having him sit around and do nothing while waiting for your return," the Demon King said. "He's a warrior. Warriors train."

Father nodded.

"Are we ready to begin?" Father asked.

"Not yet. We're waiting for others to join us."

"Others?" Father let go of Mother's hand on alert to any threat about to head our way.

An owl flew in through the open window and perched on the chair behind the King's head.

"Ah, they're almost here," the Demon King said.

Outside the door, the pounding beat of running footsteps echoed, then the door flew inward, and a woman with golden feathered wings burst into the room followed by a towering giant of a demon with leathery black wings.

"Is this them?" the woman asked.

Rexan stood. "Yes."

The woman gasped and strode closer to Mother.

"Wait." Father stood and held out a glowing hand. "Who are you and what do you want with my mate?"

The woman's wings snapped into her back and disappeared.

"I'm Thea, Queen of the Sirens. And you," she looked at Mother, then me. "Are my descendants."

"Mine as well," the hulking demon said.

"And you are?" Father asked.

"They call me Beast."

It was a very fitting name. His horns looked deadly, as did the talons on his wings, which still filled a quarter of the room.

Thea touched Mother's hand reverently. "Can you sing for me?"

Mother smiled. She loved singing almost as much as she loved Father and us children.

Fortune found,

A life worth living.
Family found,
A time of forgiving.
"Stop," Queen Thea said. "It's true. I sense every word. You have Siren's blood in you. My blood." She turned to the beast. "Our boy had children."
"So, it appears." He grinned.
"What if he's still alive?"
"My love." Beast shook his head.
"There's hope," Queen Thea said.
Mother clasped her hand. "There's always hope."
"Thank you for coming here." She turned to me. "And you, do you sing too?"
"No, I paint and write poetry."
"But you are still a descendant. Still family."
"It appears so."
The Demon King stood. "This calls for a party."
"I don't know, Rex," the Beast said.
"Melanie is dead, is she not?" Rexan asked.
"She is," Queen Thea said.
"Who's Melanie?" I asked.
"My evil twin sister. Many centuries ago, she wreaked great destruction when she unexpectedly took my place. We had to hide our son from her, but now she's dead... and you are here. It's like the stars are all aligning to bring you to me. Perhaps to bring him back home too."
"So, the rumors are true that you didn't kill my grandfather?" Father asked.
"No, I did not."

Mother's shoulders sagged lower, as though the weight of her lineage had sat heavily on them.

"Tell me how you hid your son?" Father asked.

"A lovely Fae couple raised him as their own."

"I kept track of him for years until those murderous Trappers attacked," the Beast said. "I couldn't find him afterward and assumed he'd died."

"He might still be alive," Queen Thea said, the hope glistening in her eyes made Mother reach out for her again.

"I hope you find your son," Mother said.

CHAPTER TWENTY-SIX
BRANDON

THE GUARD WHO'D FLIRTED with me burst into my room and thrust a set of clothes at me.

"Here. Dress in these." She spun away.

"What for?"

"A party." She giggled. "Save me a dance."

As if I'd dance with her. There was no other woman I wanted to dance with other than Roisin. I rushed into the bathroom, washed, and dressed. Roisin wanted me. I recognized she did. I just had to wait for her mind and heart to agree.

Before too long, a different demon guard returned and was already waiting for me with the door open. Loud music echoed up the stairs. Whatever party the demons had going on sounded like a good one. We walked down the staircase. I couldn't get there fast enough to see Roisin again. We reached the bottom floor and double doors stood open to a grand ballroom.

The guard placed his hand on my shoulder and said, "Don't do anything foolish."

"What can I possibly do?" I asked. "The only thing I understand that can hurt you is back in the bedroom that you locked."

"Keep it that way." He nodded, then strode into the party.

I was alone. Without a guard? I glanced left and then right. There were demons everywhere. I guess I didn't need a guard when anyone here could kill me when I wasn't armed with a sword to protect myself. I skirted around the edge of the ballroom. Twinkling lights fluttered along the ceiling as though a thousand magical butterfly wings were flapping in unison to the beats of the music. Demons danced in the center of the ballroom dressed in the finest garments with decadent details to rival the best of the designers back on Earth. Servers strode around the room with trays of food and drinks. Demons snatched items from the trays as they passed by. There wasn't much delicacy to these demons, but the party appeared to be entertaining.

I searched the room for Roisin, but she was nowhere to be seen. Disappointment sat heavy in my stomach. The demon guard who'd flirted with me strutted toward me in a skin-tight dress.

"Hey." She batted her eyelashes. "Let's dance."

She tugged me onto the dance floor as though I didn't have a choice. I glanced to my left, then right, wondering if I asked for help, would any of the demons step in or would they laugh? Probably the latter. I decided I'd destroy my manly image if I acted like a wimp now after beating so many in training. What was one dance?

One dance too many.

Roisin glided into the room with her royal air and the power of the Fae running through her. Even demons stopped talking to stare at her beauty. The woman I was dancing with spun me around, but I spun back so I could stare at Roisin. She wore a revealing dress that dipped down at the front to her belly button. I longed to trace the line with my tongue. The dress was a deep blue, like the sky before sunset. Which I hadn't seen for some time, but I recalled it vividly. Her gaze found mine, her lips tugged into a smile, and then her eyes landed on my dance partner. The smile fell from her lips, and she turned away from me and talked to the hulking demon beside her. I didn't know who he was, but I wanted to rip the horns from his head.

A woman in glimmering gold stepped next to the large demon, and he turned his attention to her. The look on his face was pure adulation. I sighed with relief that a demon wasn't wooing Roisin, but who was I to complain when I was getting courted myself?

The song ended and, as luck would have it, a demon pushed me aside and took the woman for the next dance. I wanted to thank him, but I strode toward Roisin. As I reached her, a man with silvery blond hair stepped in front of her. His crown of thorns writhed around his head. Holy shit, the Fae King was here.

"Your Majesty." I dipped in a bow.

Of all our training, we'd learned of the Fae King. Of the power he had. The air hummed around him as though static with energy. Power, so much power, pulsed from him. The things this King could do should make me tremble in my boots, but he was also the father of the woman I was in love with, so how should I handle that?

"You are the Fellowship member, I presume?" the Fae King asked.

"Brandon O'Cuinn, at your service." I lifted my head and met his stare.

"Brandon?" he muttered. "Roisin was quite worried about your safety here."

"Understandable, since I almost died when we arrived."

"I suppose," he said. "We'll return you to your family after the party."

"Thank you, your Majesty." I dipped in another bow.

"Niamh, my love, dance with me," the Fae King said to the beautiful woman beside him who could only be Roisin's mother as she had a similar striking beauty to her.

The Fae Queen smiled and stepped into the Fae King's arms. They danced around the ballroom as though made for the place. The giant demon took the stunning woman in the gold dress in his arms without a word and danced them across the floor, rivaling the Fae royalty.

"I don't suppose?"

"No," Roisin said.

"It meant nothing."

"What didn't?"

"Me dancing with that woman," I said. "She didn't give me much choice."

"Whatever you say." She lifted her chin.

"Roisin, don't be like that. You're the only woman in this room, hell, this kingdom, which matters to me."

"If you say so." She turned and walked out of the ballroom.

I chased after her. There was no way I'd let her go. Not now. Never. She hurried along the bottom floor of the castle, passing demons milling about in the foyer. She opened a door and disappeared into the room. I followed her, then ground to a halt inside the tiny room and laughed.

"We're in a cloak cupboard."

"I realize that now." She swiped the cloaks out of her face.

I stepped closer to her.

"There's a party going on that we should be at."

"I'd rather spend my time in here with you." I placed my hands on her waist.

She sucked in a breath through her teeth.

"Wouldn't you rather be dancing with more experienced women?"

"I couldn't care less about any other woman. Experienced or not, there's only you for me now." I stroked my thumbs over her waist.

She shivered. "Brandon, why are you making this so hard?"

"I don't mean to."

"We can't be together."

"Why not?"

"I'm a Fae Princess and you're a human Fellowship member. You'll be their leader one day."

"I'll quit the Fellowship if that's what's bothering you. I don't care about anything but you."

She laughed once, then covered her mouth as though her laughter would get us caught in here.

"It's the human part too," she said through her hand.

"What was that?" I asked, tugging her hand away from her mouth. The urge to kiss her overwhelmed me as I stared at her radiant face. "I didn't quite catch what you said."

"I said—"

Before she finished her sentence, I covered her mouth with mine. She moaned and wrapped her arms around my neck. Pressed every inch of her body into mine. I tried to break the kiss to ask her if this was what she wanted, but she kept tugging my mouth back to hers. I gave in to her demands. Traced my finger down the front of the V shape in her dress, feeling her skin pebble in goosebumps. My other hand moved lower and brushed her mound through her dress. Her entire body shook. She was so turned on that I imagined a few strokes of my finger would be all it would take to bring her to release.

Shouldn't one of us have that tonight?

I inched her dress up with my other hand until I brushed her bare mound with my fingers. She rolled her hips into my touch, chasing the pressure she so desperately needed. If she needed me, then she'd have me.

I wrenched my mouth away from hers. "Can I please touch you?"

"Aye," she said, grabbing my wrist and urging me on.

I wanted to watch, but I needed to kiss her even more. My lips found hers once again at the same time as my fingers found her damp entrance. She was dripping with desire. So slick and ready, her hips bucked into my stroking fingers. I didn't waste time finding what she liked. I rubbed the hard tip of her clitoris until her body trembled, until she was almost at that peak before the freefall of bliss. Then and only then, did I thrust two fingers inside her and made her come so hard her entire body convulsed in rapture. Her body squeezed my fingers tight, and I imagined the way she'd feel with me inside her.

My pants were so tight that each movement chafed.

Each tiny thrust of my fingers sent little aftershocks through her body until she whispered, "Enough."

I drew my fingers from her and lifted them to my mouth.

Sucking them clean, I said, "Next time I get to taste you directly."

She dropped her head back against the cloaks. The soft material looked good around her, but I'd never imagined her first orgasm from me would be in a demon cloak cupboard of all places.

I grinned and smoothed her dress back into place.

"How do you feel?"

"Good. Better." She placed her hands on my shoulders. "It was amazing having you touch me that way, but it's more than that." She shook her head. "I can't explain it."

"Try."

"It's like I'm meant to be with you, yet I realize that's not true."

"Why? Because I'm human?"

"Aye. Fae can't mark a human as their mate because the power will kill them."

"I'm aware. It's in our studies."

"So why do you want to be with me?"

"Because I love everything about you. Can't that be enough?"

"Perhaps," she said and pointed at the door. "I should leave first. Mother and Father are probably wondering where I am."

"Yeah, I probably have demons looking for me, too."

I kissed her forehead. "I'll see you in the ballroom and maybe this time you'll dance with me."

"Perhaps you might be lucky." She smiled.

"Luckiest man here." I winked.

She opened the door and disappeared back to the party. I had no clue what it was celebrating, and I didn't care. So long as Roisin was out there, I'd be there too.

CHAPTER TWENTY-SEVEN

ROISIN

I SWEAR I WAS blushing the entire time I was at the party after Brandon had given me an orgasm in the cloakroom. Demon after demon had asked me to dance, and I couldn't say no because I was so happy, elated even. Who knew having a man give you an orgasm made you feel this way? No wonder my sisters were so happy with their fated mates if they were getting orgasms like the one I'd just experienced.

Tay sent me a wink as she danced past me.

The Demon King himself danced with me.

The hulking Beast was next.

"Your mother said you're her youngest child," the Beast said.

He was so enormous it was hard to keep up with him.

"I am."

"And your father's favorite."

I laughed. "That's what everyone says."

"And what's your opinion?"

"On what?"

"Whatever you'd like to say."

"Hmm, no one has ever asked me that."

"You're my great-grandchild, not sure how many greats are in there, but I, we'd like to get to know you."

"No offense, but you're very intimidating."

He smirked. "I worked hard to get that."

"Queen Thea too."

"She worked hard too. It's difficult ruling powerful people. I'm sure your father would say the same thing. It's probably even harder for him being a father to so many powerful offspring."

"I suppose." I glanced over at my father, who was now dancing with Queen Thea.

"What happened to your son?"

"We left him in the care of a Fae couple because the Autumn Court was too dangerous a place for him with Thea's sister alive. She was evil and twisted. Crazy. Saltine would check on him occasionally and then tell me, but after the Trappers attacked the Fae, she never returned. We assumed he'd died."

"You're close with Saltine?"

"I wouldn't say that. She agreed to help me instead of me killing her."

"Why did you want to kill her? From what I've heard of the witch seer, she's only helped people."

"Long story that involved my imprisonment." He picked me up and twirled me around as though I were as light as a feather.

I squealed, then laughed. He lowered me back to my feet.

"Saltine is a priestess, not a witch seer."

"Why would she tell us she was a witch seer?"

"Beats me." He shrugged. "Things change. The different realms believe different things to what once was. She's older than me, so she probably adapted to the changes in time. Perhaps that's why she called herself a witch seer."

"I suppose. It would be nice to meet her one day and ask her."

He chuckled. "Believe me, if you meet her, then you better be ready for whatever she says is coming your way, because she's never wrong. I guess that's the perk of being a bridge between the divine and having foresight."

If I ever met Saltine, would she tell me when I'd meet my fated mate? I glanced around the ballroom. Why hadn't I seen Brandon return after our intimate moment in the cloak closet? A nervous energy bounced inside my stomach and my power flared to my hands. The Beast glanced at the ice covering my palms.

"Problem?" he asked, not missing a step of the dance.

"I'm not sure. The human guard who came with me was here and now I can't find him."

"Why is a human here?"

"I accidentally brought him with me the first time I came."

"Come on." He stopped dancing and grabbed my hand, taking me across the dance floor to the Demon King. "Rex, the human, have you seen him?"

Rexan frowned. "Not for some time. The last I saw him, he was chasing Roisin here out of the ballroom."

My cheeks heated. "He didn't come back in?"

"No." The Demon King clicked his fingers, and a demon rushed to his side. He whispered in his ear, and the demon shook his head. "He hasn't come back inside the ballroom."

"But he promised he'd follow me back inside."

Brandon would never break his promise to me. Too much time had passed since I'd left him in the cloak cupboard for him not to be here. For me to not sense him looking at me. Why hadn't I noticed sooner he wasn't in the room?

"Then where is he?"

"Relax, he can't leave the Winter Court," Rexan said.

"We have to find him," I said urgently.

"We will. He can't have gone far," Rexan said. "I'll send a search party through the castle. They'll find him."

"What if a demon hurt him?"

"He's quite a formidable opponent. We would have heard a fight."

"What if they dragged him outside? We wouldn't have heard that."

I didn't say the rest. What if he was freezing to death while we'd been dancing and having a grand party? What if I failed to take him home to his family?

And what if...

The man I'd fallen for died before I admitted I loved him?

CHAPTER TWENTY-EIGHT
BRANDON

A GROAN ECHOED INSIDE my head. Wait, that was my groan, and that pain was in my head. What happened? I lifted my hand and touched my throbbing skull, then peeled my eyes open. A blurry thatched roof was all I saw. Voices mumbled to the right of me. I rolled over, and a sudden wave of nausea churned my stomach. My hand roamed to the back of my head and my fingers found sticky goo stuck to my hair. Blood. Someone had hit me on the head. So hard that it had knocked me out and made me bleed.

I forced my eyes to focus on the two people talking across the room. They wavered in and out of focus for a few minutes while the churning in my stomach eased. The old man came into focus, as did the demon woman who'd flirted with me, the one who'd forced me to dance.

"He's awake," the old man said, stumbling over to me on his cane. "Why did you hit him so hard?"

The demon shrugged. "We had a deal, Niall. How I got the human here wasn't part of it."

"What's going on?" The words weren't like my own. They came out slurred and quiet.

"We need to talk. I have little time left." His gnarled hand hovered in front of my face then he turned and picked up a mortar and pestle. "Let me heal you first."

"No." I struggled to sit, but I did it. My head swam, and the room tilted sideways, but then it righted itself.

He placed the mortar and pestle on the table. "Son, please."

"I'm not your son. You're insane."

"There's only one way you'll believe me, isn't there? You'll need to see for yourself." The old man bobbed his head as though agreeing with himself.

"Vizz, carry him to the forest."

The demon stared at the old man like he'd lost his mind, but I already recognized he had. She strode toward me, and I kicked my legs in her face, but the fuzziness in my eyes and the dizziness in my head made my aim less than accurate. She grabbed my ankles and wrapped them with ropes. I swung my fists at her head, connecting a few times before she tied my wrists together too. She picked me up and flung me over her shoulder. Blood rushed to my aching head, and I moaned and then passed out again.

The cold outside brought me back to consciousness in an instant. My body bounced on the demon's shoulder, making the nausea impossible to deal with. I retched into the snow. She grumbled but didn't stop walking.

"Here," the old man said.

She stopped and dropped me on the ground. "You're a lunatic, Niall. The wolves in the forest will more than likely kill him."

"No, he's my son. He has to see my memory to understand."

Niall was my father's name. Was this crazy old fool right? Was I his son? Or was he pretending to be him? He had to be crazy. How could I see his memory?

I shivered as the cold of the snow seeped into my body.

"Cut him loose," Niall said.

Vizz scowled but slid a knife from a holster and stepped toward me. The blade glinted in the sunlight. I inched backward toward the trees. That knife looked deadlier than the forest. The knife slid through the ropes at my feet. I kicked the demon in the face and sprinted into the forest, ducking and weaving through the snow-laden branches. My head hurt with every beat of my heart, but I wouldn't let that crazy old man and the demon kill me. Not when I'd had a taste of Roisin.

Not when she'd let me experience her ecstasy on my fingers.

I had too much to live for, and it was Roisin.

All for her.

I ran and ran, not even knowing which direction I was heading. It was foolish and the longer I ran, the less my head hurt until sense kicked in and I stopped and listened. No footfalls followed me. I was alone in the forest. The cold penetrated my fear. I shivered and blew warm air on my tied hands.

Okay, time to head back to the castle. I turned a full circle, but snow-laden trees were the only thing in existence. Well, shit, I'd have to follow my footsteps back the way I'd run. That was the only option, otherwise I'd get lost in here if I wasn't already. First, I needed to free my hands because if those idiots were still waiting, then I needed to fight them off. Who knows what else they had in store for me?

I slowly walked back the way I'd run, searching every inch of the snow-covered forest for a way to cut off the ropes. My foot kicked something hard under the snow. I dropped to my knees and dug as best as possible with my tied hands eventually unearthing a rock. Better than anything else I'd found. I rubbed the rope back and forth on the rock, hoping it was sharp enough to cut my bindings.

My fingers grew numb, then my hands, but I kept sawing my arms back and forth until the ropes gave a little, then a lot, and my hands fell apart as the ropes tumbled to the snowy ground. I staggered to my feet. Every inch of my body was growing numb with the icy cold around me. The fancy clothes for the ball did nothing to protect me against the elements of the Winter Court. I'd grown up in Ireland where it was cold, but this place was extreme.

I forced my legs to the nearest tree and tugged on the branch hoping to rip it off to use as a weapon, but the second I touched it, my head swam with a vision.

A tiny baby swaddled in a thick blanket. A beautiful woman rocking the baby in her arms. She lifted her head and smiled.

"There you are, Niall, I was thinking you'd got lost," my mother said.

"I'm here," my father said.

Niall looked exactly like the photos in our home. He was handsome. The same coloring as me. Everyone said I looked just like him and here he was in my mind, alive and well. I longed to reach out and hug him.

He crossed the room and wrapped her in his arms, cradling me, too. "I love you both so very much."

"I love you too, and young Brandon will grow up loving you."

"My beautiful wife, I wish I could be here to see that."

"What do you mean?" Mother frowned.

"I made a mistake. I learned a secret that I shouldn't have. You appreciate how I am. How I go digging until I have to learn everything. I wish I could take it all back now, so I'd be here with you both." He stepped backward. "I discovered the source of the magical bookshelf in the library. The source of the Fellowship."

Mother placed me in a bassinet.

"Niall, please, tell me what's going on." She stepped toward him, but the Demon King materialized between them. She gasped and raced back to the bassinet, putting herself between me and the demon.

"I said to say goodbye, not tell her the secrets," the Demon King said.

"I didn't tell her," Niall said.

"No?" The Demon King's eyes blazed with power. "You were about to, though. I can't trust you, Niall. This is the only way to keep the secret."

The Demon King stepped closer to Mother and snatched her in his arms. She screamed, but he lowered his head and drew her scream into his mouth. Magic sparked dark and deadly in the air. Mother's eyes rolled back into her head, and she collapsed in his arms. The Demon King lowered her to the ground.

"What did you do to her?"

"I removed this memory. You were supposed to say goodbye, and that was all, but now she won't even have that to look back on fondly." He stepped toward Father. "I gave you an option, Niall, and yet you chose the hard way. It would be easier if I killed you now."

"No," Father said. "Please let me live. Let me live knowing my son is growing into a fine young man even though I'll never see it."

"The Winter Court is a death sentence for a human, anyway." The Demon King clasped Father's arm and created a portal.

They vanished.

My eyes snapped open. It was true, the old man was my father, and I'd refused to believe it. Refused to spend time with him while I'd had the chance. No wonder he'd grown desperate and forced me to accept the truth. What was this place? How had it shown me this memory? I stared at all the trees, not daring to touch any of them. I'd failed to pull a branch free, but my hands were bloody as though I'd left bits of my flesh on the branch. They stung too. I wiped them on my snow-covered clothes.

I glanced up. Snow was falling, and I'd failed to even notice while in that magical memory. It lay thick on my clothes. The cold seeping into my aching head was like a soothing balm, but this was more than likely to kill me. How long had I been in that memory? My limbs ached and barely moved when I tried to stand. I stared at the fading footprints in the snow, then dragged myself on my hands and knees. Inch by frozen inch I'd make my way out of here.

I'd find my father and hug him. Tell him I understood it wasn't his fault that he'd left us. Tell him I love him.

Then I'd find Roisin with whatever strength I had left to make it to the castle. I'd find her and tell her I love her, and she was free to find her fated mate. Free to be with her destined love, because I was dying a slow, agonizing death and she'd live forever.

Forever without me.

The way it was supposed to be for a Fae.

And I was merely a human.

She deserved to be happy. I'd tell her that with my last breath.

CHAPTER TWENTY-NINE

ROISIN

"H E'S NOT IN THE castle," the Demon King said.

"Then where is he?" Father asked, having joined us.

"I've sent a search party outside," the Demon King said.

"I'm going too."

"We'll all go," Father said. "The Fellowship member is all of our responsibility."

"Agreed," the Demon King said. "Secrets no longer need to be kept. I won't have the young man die here. I'll return him to Earth myself as soon as we find him."

He glanced at Tay, who scowled but nodded. There was more they weren't telling us, but I didn't care about anything else except finding Brandon. We strode out the doors of the castle and immediately two guards flew to the King, landing in front of him.

"Your Majesty, we believe he's in the Forest of Forgetting."

"No," the Demon King said. His wings snapped out, and he launched into the sky, leaving us staring after him.

"Where's the forest?" I asked.

The guard shook his head. "You can't go into the forest."

"Why not?" Father asked.

"You don't want to go into the forest," the other guard said.

"At least take us near the forest," Father said. "We'll wait on the outskirts for the King to return with the man."

Mother slid her arm through Father's and gave him her concerned look, but I agreed with Father that the closer we were to the forest the better, so we'd see if the King brought Brandon out and returned him home. The icy air whipped around us as we walked away from the castle. Brandon was human, and he'd almost died from exposure to the cold in the Winter Court. How long had he been outside? It was so hard to tell the time in this place. It was so different to the Summer Court and Earth.

The walk was a long one, and every step was crucial to getting Brandon inside and out of the cold. Tay would heal him again if he'd suffered frostbite, I was sure of that, so I didn't worry about him losing limbs. He had to be all right. My heart ached if I thought he wouldn't be all right.

There was no other choice. I loved the man. I wanted more time with him than these fleeting moments we'd shared.

We arrived at the edge of the forest where quite an array of demons had converged. In the center of them stood a hunched-over old man. Another human? I thought they didn't like humans in the Winter Court.

"Who is the old man?" I asked the guard.

The guard looked at me but didn't answer. The old man was crying and blabbering incoherently. A woman demon had her arms wrapped around him, comforting him, which was a strange sight to see, because demons appeared to despise humans, or perhaps they only looked down on them?

A howl of wolves rang out from the forest.

"Shit," the guard said.

All the other demons froze and stared into the forest.

"Now what?"

"There are guardian demon wolves in the forest. That's why no one goes in there."

"What about the Demon King?"

"He's the ruler, of course, he goes anywhere in his realm."

"So, if he finds Brandon before the wolves, then he'll be fine," I said, trying to convince myself more than the demon.

The demon's lips firmed into a tight line. Huge leathery wings and a set of golden feathered wings circled the forest overhead. The Beast and Queen Thea had joined the search. I was suddenly thankful for the extra family members. The Beast growled high in the sky, but an answering growl came from the forest. Then the Beast and Queen Thea flew to us and dropped from the sky.

"He has him," the Beast said, as he stood in front of me, a giant of a demon, blocking my view of the forest.

I bounced left, then right, trying to look behind him.

The Beast placed his hands on my shoulders and looked me in the eye. "It's not good."

"No." I gasped, my power surged, and shot ice into him, breaking his hold on me. I ducked under his arm and ran toward the forest.

My parents called out my name, and the demons yelled, but no one would stop me. I threw up a blockade of ice behind me. I heard it crumble a second later, whether at the hands of my father, or the Beast, I wasn't sure, but I kept running toward the forest. A dark shadow appeared. The tall form of the Demon King stepped from the last of the trees in the forest. He carried something in his arms.

Brandon.

I ran even faster.

The Demon King paused outside the edge of the forest and placed Brandon on the ground.

"No, no, no." I skidded to a stop by his side and dropped to the ground. "Brandon."

His skin was blue from his lips to his cheeks. Ice covered his eyelashes. He appeared to be a sleeping ice sculpture. My hands landed on his chest hoping against hope that his heart still beat, that he wasn't dead yet.

There.

A tiny faint flicker of a heartbeat.

"He's not dead."

"Not yet." The Demon King grimaced.

A hand landed on my shoulder, then the old man fell across Brandon's body.

"My son, I didn't mean to hurt you. I just wanted you to see the truth."

"Son?" I shoved the old man from Brandon. "You did this to him and he's your son!"

My power flared. I wanted to kill him for hurting Brandon. Make him suffer for the death that Brandon was about to experience.

"Dad?" Brandon's voice croaked.

I jolted to a stop. The old man crawled back to Brandon's side.

"Son, I'm so sorry."

"It's okay, Dad." Brandon shivered.

The old man touched Brandon's frozen cheek.

"At least I understand you didn't leave me on purpose," Brandon struggled to get out as though each word was painful. His blue lips cracked and bled with each movement of his lips.

"Brandon, I love you, son."

"I love you too." Brandon's eyes fluttered closed.

"I didn't mean for you to run into the forest." He sobbed. "I only wanted you to see I didn't want to leave you."

I couldn't lose Brandon like this. He was mortal, but he deserved a full mortal life, not the few years he'd enjoyed. My power built and built until I wasn't able to contain it any longer. The Veil heeded my call and swirled into existence.

"Roisin, stop," Father said.

"No, I promised I'd take him home and I will."

Father's eyes glittered with pride, but he shook his head. "The Veil might kill him."

Tears fell from my eyes and instantly turned to icicles.

"He's dying, anyway."

Snow swept around Brandon's body, lifting him into the air. I drew on my power to walk with him into the Veil, but I couldn't do it. I couldn't be the one to end his suffering. My hand snapped into my pocket where I'd kept Tay's stone. If Tay imbued it with her demon magic, then it was a demon portal, and it might work as a gateway to wherever I wanted. I yanked it out and said the words she'd told me to say.

The Veil vanished, and a portal took its place. Placing my hand into the swirling snow of my powers hovering Brandon's body in the air, I stepped into the portal. The trip was instantaneous. One second, I was in the Winter Court, the next I was in the secluded garden of the Fellowship beside the spring. I lowered Brandon to the ground and drew my power back until no speck of snow covered him, but he was still. Silent. Blue and bloody.

A scream rent the air, and then his mother was shaking him and crying. Brandon's body flopped with each heart-wrenching movement.

"Please, do something." She lifted her tear-streaked face to mine.

My tears had fallen silent and unheeded until the moment devastation stared back at me.

"I'm not sure what to do. I'm not a healer. My power is over ice, not fire. The cold of the Winter Court did this to him. I'd unfreeze him if I could." I held out my hands. "Tell me what to do, please."

"He's my boy. I love him," she sobbed.

"I love him too."

"Then save him. Do anything."

Behind me, the water trickled down the fountain, kicking my frozen brain into gear.

"If we were in the Summer Court, I'd try the water from the Spring of Life... your fountain has the same water..." I walked closer to the fountain. "What if?"

"No," she said. "The water corrupts humans. He'd rather be dead than like a Trapper."

I put my hand in the water. Power thrummed over my skin. This was the answer. The only answer to saving Brandon.

"It's the only way to save him."

"I said no." She stood and marched over to me.

My power lashed out from my palms in an instant, wrapping her legs in ice so she couldn't stop me.

"You wanted me to do anything to save him," I reminded her. "This is it."

I scooped the water into my hand and carried it back to Brandon. He was so lifeless, but tiny droplets of blood still spilled from his lips and his bloodied hands, whatever had happened to them. I lifted the back of his head and gently tipped the handful of water into his mouth. He didn't swallow at first, but then he did. I gathered his head into my lap and stroked his hair, watching and waiting to see if the water from the spring would heal a human.

Time ticked. His mother cursed me the entire time. Other Fellowship members came to investigate the noise, but I froze their legs too. No one would get near Brandon while I was here.

Father and Mother stepped through the Veil and kneeled beside me.

"Roisin, sweetheart," Mother said.

"No," I said, placing my hand on his chest.

I couldn't lose him. My heart ached. Every inch of my body howled in pain. There would be nothing for me if I didn't have Brandon. I understood that deep in my core.

Ice covered my hands. It flowed onto Brandon and the ground, and soon my magical ice encased everyone in the garden and held them in a state of stasis. Alive but not moving. It wasn't enough. My power screamed at me to fix Brandon. To bring him back to me and if it couldn't, then to freeze it all until I figured out how to do so. On and on it poured, freezing anything and everything in its path.

Brandon was mine.

Death wouldn't take him from me.

CHAPTER THIRTY

ROISIN

I CE CRUNCHED UNDER FOOTSTEPS. How? I thought I'd frozen everything.

"Well, you certainly have some Rage Demon in you," Tay said.

I turned around and found her standing with the Demon King and the Beast. I suppose my family had arrived to help me, but no one could bring a human back from the dead.

And Brandon was dead.

I realized in the depths of my heart.

"Your parents won't stay frozen long," the Demon King said.

"It doesn't matter. Nothing matters now he's gone."

The Beast smiled. A strange thing to do in this situation.

"Demons have fated mates too," he said.

"So," I said shrugging. I couldn't care less about whoever the fates sent me now. I only wanted Brandon and his cocky attitude. His teasing smile. The way he looked at me like I was the only woman alive in all the realms.

A laugh cackled through the silent world, and then a woman in a cloak materialized in a smokey swirl of magic.

"Saltine," the Beast said, "what do we owe you for now?"

"You don't owe me anything." She drew the hood back from her head. "Everything is as it should be."

I lurched to my feet. "Everything is as it should be!" I blasted her with a jolt of ice straight to her chest.

The blow didn't even move her. Her emerald eyes glittered.

"Watch it, young one, or I won't help your mate."

"Mate?"

"You marked him as yours when you threw your little tantrum." She waved her hand around the iciness of Earth.

"Marked?" I shook my head. I didn't remember putting my mark on his chest. Surely I'd remember that... but if I did...

"Did I kill Brandon?" I gasped. Had the spring water helped him, but I'd killed him?

"He's not quite dead, yet."

"What? How?"

"You fed him water from the spring. It protected him against your powers. Stopped them from killing him."

"So, he'll wake? He'll live?"

"Live, yes, wake, that's a matter of you undoing this freeze."

"I'm not sure how I did it."

"You're powerful. All you Fae are."

"Hey," the Beast said.

"Demons are different." She flicked him a narrowed glance. "But yes, powerful too. Did that satisfy your ego, Beast?"

The Beast shrugged.

"So, if I figure out how to unfreeze everything, I'll have Brandon back? And as my mate, no less?"

Had all my dreams come true?

Her eyes rolled back into her head and the whites flickered back and forth from side to side.

"What's happening?"

"She's having a vision," the Demon King said.

"Wait!" Her eyes snapped into place. "No." She glanced to the left, then the right.

A burst of thunder cracked the air. Smoke billowed around her body.

"Saltine, don't you dare move!" came a thundering voice from the sky.

A second later, a tall man appeared before us dressed in an immaculate pin-striped suit and top hat, an ornate cane graced his long fingers.

"Father." She bowed to the ground.

"Rise, child." He tutted. "What mischief have you been up to?"

"I'm helping where you would not," she said, rising.

I glanced over at the demons, but they called on a portal and vanished.

"Helping?" He tapped his cane on the ice, cracking it with each tiny blow.

"You would have let all your creations die. I was ensuring they lived and lived happily."

"You have too much of your witch mother in you." He clicked his tongue. "She always wanted to help anyone."

"You're just angry she didn't want to stay in the Heavens with you."

"Dia?" I muttered in awe.

"Yes, child?" The man faced me.

I dropped to the ground in a curtsy. Our God was in front of us. And Saltine called him father? Wait... Pepper, Lorcan's mate, was related to Saltine. That meant Pepper was related to God. No wonder she'd survived Lorcan's mating mark when we'd all thought she was a mortal witch. We'd assumed it was her wolf shifter heritage that had kept her alive, but this new revelation made more sense. My gaze darted to Brandon. Was he related to God too?

"No, child, this young man is human alone," he said as though reading my thoughts.

"But Saltine said I could save him."

"Doubtful. He's too far gone from this world to save."

"Please, Dia, I can't lose him."

"And what would you offer to save him?"

"Anything."

Dia glanced around at all the frozen people. "Would you kill them all to save one?"

I gasped. "No, that's not right."

"So let him go then."

"No." I rose to my feet. "He did nothing wrong but fall in love with a Fae Princess. He shouldn't die because of me. Take me instead."

"Take me instead she says as if it was that easy to swap lives."

Saltine slowly backed away while we were talking.

"I suppose my daughter has worked hard to save so many, it would be a shame to see her efforts go to waste now after all these years." His gaze snapped to Saltine. "Daughter, what do you suppose I should do?"

"You'll do whatever you want, Father."

"That's right, and what I want is for you to come home to the Heavens and fulfill your destiny."

Saltine shook her head. "My destiny is here in these realms just as Mother's was."

A puff of smoke exploded around her, and then she vanished.

"That child of mine." He sighed. "I have a perfectly suitable God picked out for her and what does she do? Play matchmaker in these realms." He walked over to Brandon and kneeled next to him. "And he is her latest with you."

"I..." My mind whirled with all that had happened. Dia was here. Saltine was his daughter. "I love him, and he loves me even though we aren't fated mates."

"Who do you suppose makes fated mates?" He smirked.

My breath puffed out into the cold air.

"You can make him mine?"

"He was always meant to be yours." He tore open Brandon's shirt. "You already marked him as yours."

"But he's still dying."

"This was how it was supposed to be. Saltine foresaw him as your fated mate for a reason. And that reason is me. I make your fated mates. I make Fae." He placed the handle of his cane on Brandon's forehead. "You and your family will fix this mess you made of Earth. I'm quite fond of this realm. I have to say I've been very disappointed in the way you abandoned it."

"We'll fix it. We'll stay and never abandon Earth again."

"Very well." The cane on Brandon's forehead glowed a bright red with the godly power of Dia rolling into him. Mending him and letting him live.

The magic circled his head in a radiant red glow. Round and round it fluctuated and then slowly ebbed back into Dia's cane. I gasped. On Brandon's head was a crown of thorns. A Fae royal crown.

"There you go." Dia stood and stretched his arms over his head, lifting the cane, too. Another crack of thunder exploded in the sky even though there had been no lightning. "He is your fated mate."

"And Fae royalty."

"The crown was all your doing when you marked him."

"Female Fae don't have the power to give our mates crowns."

"You do if you want to, and your mate wants it. You both must have wanted it."

"I did." I'd longed for Brandon to not be human. To be my fated mate.

"Well, let me fix one more thing first." He lifted the cane into the air and sent a red flare into the sky. It exploded like a star and sent tiny drops back down to Earth. I was the only one around to see this. Would anyone believe me?

"What else did you fix?"

"Humans believe in Fae again. They'll treat you with respect and we'll have none of that nonsense the Trappers tried, I promise you that. You'll live in peace and harmony as I first intended."

He vanished as quickly as he'd arrived, leaving me standing in a sea of frozen people. I forced my power into the ice, wanting to undo the damage I'd caused in my emotional state, but nothing happened. Except the ice fell away from Brandon. My fated mate. Brandon sat up and looked around.

"What the hell happened now?"

CHAPTER THIRTY-ONE
BRANDON

ROSIN RAN AT ME and dove into me, knocking me back onto the icy ground. My head hit the ice and bounced, but it didn't hurt the way it had before I'd passed out in the forest. Was I still in the Winter Court? It looked like I was with all the ice and snow around me. I lifted a hand and touched my head, but thorns pricked my fingers.

"Ow," I said, pulling my hand back. "What's on my head?"

"A crown." Roisin grinned.

"Why am I wearing a crown?"

"I'm not sure you'll believe me."

"Believe what?" I couldn't keep from staring at her. From having her in my arms where I'd dreamed she was. But wait, my dreams had been of her as a child. "I saw you grow up."

She kept smiling. "Aye. I marked you as my mate and you would have seen my memories."

"Seen your memories?" I touched my head again. "I'm so confused. The last thing I remember was seeing my mother's memory of the day my father left us. The old man in the cottage in the Winter Court is my father."

"I saw him." Her lips pulled into a grim line.

"I need to talk to him." I sat up. "Where are we?" I noticed the frozen people around us. "Why is everyone encased in ice?"

"We're on Earth. You were dying, and I'd promised to take you home." Her eyes glistened with unshed tears. "I lost control of my powers when I thought you'd die and leave me." Two tears spilled from the corners of her eyes. "All I wanted was to stop you from dying, and then I somehow encased everyone in magical ice to stop that happening." She hung her head. "I froze the entire Earth into a state of stasis and I don't know how to undo it."

I drew her into my chest and hugged her. "We'll figure it out."

"We?"

"You said I'm your mate, didn't you?"

She lifted a hand between our chests and traced the new lines on it. "I marked you as my mate, and now I'll be able to track you anywhere. Never will I let anyone hurt you again, but then again, you're immortal now. You're Fae royalty."

"What?" I shifted her off my lap and stood.

"It's why you have a crown." She bit her lip.

"I need a mirror."

I edged closer to the frozen spring, needing to see for myself. My shirt hung open and an intricate swirl of knots sat etched into my skin over my heart. I traced the lines with a reverent finger as though I sensed Roisin in every line and mark placed on me. My gaze snapped to my head where a crown of thorns circled my hair. The thorns moved as though alive. My hand shook as I touched it. Power surged to my palms, and they glowed a magical sky blue.

"I have powers too?" My mouth fell open.

"I'm sorry," she whispered into the icy stillness of the garden.

"What are my powers?"

"I'm not sure, Dia didn't say."

"Dia?"

"Aye. Dia—God."

"God was here?"

"Our God."

"Our God. I'm not human anymore. I'm Fae. With powers." The words came out strangely as I absorbed the enormity of my change.

"Aye."

My gaze landed on Roisin. "And you marked me as your mate."

"I did."

"You love me."

"I love you." She gave me a tentative smile. "Are you angry?"

I frowned. "Why would I be angry?"

"You didn't consent to any of this."

"I would have died, and I'd rather be anything, even one of those scary-looking demons, so long as I got to spend eternity with you." I walked across the icy garden, trying not to slip. "The cold doesn't bother me anymore."

"It won't now you're Fae."

"I love it," I said, grinning. "But I love you more."

She threw her arms around my neck as soon as I was close enough to her. I caught her and dragged her into my body. We slipped on the ice and then landed on the ground. Capturing her face between my palms, I kissed her quickly.

"I could lay here forever with you, but how do we help free everyone?"

"I'm not sure. Mother and Father will free themselves soon so I can ask them."

"Back to the books while we wait?"

"Aye."

We climbed to our feet and hurried toward the underground library. She'd frozen the stairs too and each step down was precarious, but I was now immortal. I couldn't wrap my head around the fact I'd never die. How would I lead the Fellowship now I was a Fae? Would all of my training have been for nothing in the end? Or would this bring the humans and Fae closer together?

The sight before me made me stop at the bottom of the stairs. She'd frozen the table and chairs. Even every single book she'd frozen into an icy sculpture. I inched closer to the table and picked up a book. Crystal flakes of ice fell from the frozen pages. I tried lifting a corner, but the paper broke.

"We can't read any of these." I set the book back on the table. "How will we help everyone? What if they die before we help them?"

"They won't die," Roisin said. "It's the one thing I'm certain about. I was trying to save you. My powers were trying to do my bidding even when I was too overcome with anguish at the idea of losing you to control them."

"You're sure."

"Aye. Dia wants me to fix my mess, so it's doable."

"I guess all we can do is wait for your parents to unfreeze and hope they can help you."

"They will. My parents are older and wiser than me." She pursed her lips. "I suppose this is one time being young has its disadvantages."

I let out a half-relieved breath and half chuckle and closed the distance between us. The connection with Roisin was even greater now. My body hummed to be nearer to her. The mark on my chest warmed.

We kissed with a desperate need to show each other how much we loved each other. I might have secretly wished I was anything but human so I'd have more time with Roisin, but never would I have imagined I'd become Fae like her.

There was no better place to be with her than in this icy world right now. We couldn't do anything to help the Fellowship and my family until we had more knowledge. This small moment in time alone was ours. Her powers were ice. She thought she was ice, but she was fire and burning me up to be inside her.

My lips trailed to her neck, and she moaned.

"Roisin," I whispered. "If I don't make you mine, I might go insane."

She giggled. "We can't have an insane Fae royal, can we?"

She lifted my hand and placed it over her heart. "This is where you'll mark me, but not today. We need to fix everything first."

"Okay."

Our lips met again as though we couldn't kiss each other enough. Somehow, her back ended up on the desk, my body falling on top of hers. Neither of us noticed anything around us while we were kissing.

"Can I worship your body?"

She tugged her bottom lip into her mouth and then nodded. I kissed my way down her neck, over the delicate skin of her collarbone, reveling in the tiny goosebumps pebbling her flesh. My hands stroked her body as I inched my way down, touching, stroking, and caressing every part of her through her clothes. Nothing mattered but her. I dropped to my knees and inched her dress higher and higher, kissing and stroking her legs until I inhaled her sweet aroma, then set to work worshipping her most intimate place with my tongue. Each swipe sent an incoherent sound from her mouth, and it spurred me on even more to give her more pleasure. Her thigh muscles grew tight against the side of my head. My crown of thorns had to be digging into her, but she was too far gone in the thralls of passion to care. The next swipe of my tongue sent her over the edge, and she came so hard she coated my mouth and chin in her release. I swallowed it like a starving man.

I placed soft kisses on her stomach and hips as I rose and kissed her parted lips. She didn't care about tasting herself on my lips. She returned my kiss with the same enthusiasm as before. I loved her so much. She was perfect for me. Now she was fated to be mine forever.

"I want to make you mine too," I said.

"When you mark me, I'll fall into the Quiet while I absorb your memories. No one knows how long it'll last. I'm surprised you woke so soon after I marked you, but maybe Dia turning you Fae helped speed up the process."

My palms glowed with my new powers, but I nodded my head. Making love to her would have to be enough for now because she still needed to unfreeze everyone.

"As soon as you unfreeze Earth, you're mine."

"I'm yours now. Nothing can come between us."

"Nothing but my pants." I winked, trying to lighten the heaviness of the enormity of our recent problems.

Her gaze drank in my body like a person dying of thirst in the desert. We were far from the dessert, but the comparison was still the same.

As I stood between her spread legs, I trailed my hands up her legs and watched her skin pebble once again and her muscles quiver. My fingers trembled with the enormity of our first time as I unbuckled my pants. She was so perfect, even when she thought she wasn't. My cock sprung free and slid along her slickness. Her back arched as though she enjoyed the sensation of my body against hers. As though she, too, was battling the magnitude of our first time together. Slowly, I pushed the tip of my cock inside her and then waited. Her hands lifted to my arms and tugged on them, urging me on.

"Do it," she said. "Make me yours and only yours in this way."

I let go of my control and seated myself fully inside her. She gasped. I groaned. The sounds echoed off the icy library, making a different type of music. Music just for us. The connection was instantaneous, as though being inside her was right. The answer to every question in the universe. There was only her and me. Fated. Loved.

Mates.

I understood the enormity of fated mates now.

Our lips met again in a passionate kiss. Our bodies moved in sync. Each thrust of my hips made her gasp with pleasure. Each slide of my cock along her tight walls made my balls tighten with the impending explosion of our passion. I wasn't sure how long I made love to her, but it didn't matter. All that mattered was the pleasure we were both experiencing. The love we were sharing. The future we were making together.

"Brandon." She thrashed her head from side to side, saying my name in a plea. "Brandon."

"I got you." I licked my thumb and lowered it to the hard tip of her clit.

Her legs jerked with the contact, then her entire body shook and she screamed her release. The ice shattered around us and landed on us, on the floor, everywhere. I kept thrusting into her. chasing my release as her inner walls pulsed against me. I let go and flew with her into the pinnacle of ecstasy. On and on, my cock emptied into her. Filled her. Marked her inside as mine forever.

Our lips parted. Our breaths heaved along with our chests. She grinned at me with a well-loved expression that I wanted to see on her delicate features for the rest of our immortal lives. I smiled back at her with all the love in my body for the amazing woman she was.

"I comprehend how to get rid of the ice."

I dropped my head onto the crunchy ice on the desk beside her. "Way to ruin a man's ego over your first time."

She placed dainty kisses on my neck and the side of my face, telling me with her body how much her first time with me meant.

"There are no words to describe my first time with you." She placed her hands on my chest and urged me up so she could stare into my eyes. "I'll paint it instead."

"Yeah?"

"Aye. I'll be painting a lot of you in the future."

"Naked?" I asked with a teasing grin.

She laughed. "Let me fix my mistake first."

"Hey." I tugged her up from the desk and fixed our clothes. "You didn't make a mistake."

"It feels like I did."

"You didn't. It's fate. All this brought us together. There's no mistake in that."

CHAPTER THIRTY-TWO

ROISIN

B RANDON WAS RIGHT. I couldn't consider anything that I'd done as a mistake because it had resulted in him becoming a Fae. In him being my fated mate. We dressed and hurried outside. What I had in mind would take a wide-open space to perform.

I had it in my blood. I just had to tap into the power of the Sirens.

We walked back to the fountain. Inside, the ice sculptures of Mother and Father were twitching, their powers too great to be held forever by my magic. Could they see Brandon and me through the ice? Their eyes were open, and I was suddenly glad we'd had sex in the library where there was no one around.

"What's the plan?" Brandon asked.

"Singing."

"Singing?"

"Downstairs, when I made that noise," I whispered. "I cracked the ice."

His eyes lit with understanding.

"My Fae powers create ice, but the Siren powers in my blood cracked it downstairs."

"It's worth a shot, otherwise we'll need an enormous flamethrower to reheat Earth," he joked, trying to lighten the mood in the way he always did with his teasing ways.

"What is a flamethrower?"

"One day I'll show you all Earth offers."

"And I'll show you the Summer Court and all its magical beauty."

"I need to go back to the Winter Court and talk to my father, too."

"Of course. I'd like to visit the Autumn Court and my Siren relatives, too."

"We're going to have a lot of traveling in our future."

"We are," I said. "Will we ever settle?"

"You're my home. Wherever you are, then that's good enough for me."

I pressed a quick kiss to his lips. "Good enough for me too. Besides, who wants to live forever in one place?"

Brandon laughed. "You lived fifty years in the Summer Court."

"True, but I didn't have a choice. Now we do. All of us do."

"Are we going to stand here and talk all day? Because I'd like to put a mating mark on your chest." He leaned closer and whispered, "Can I do it while I'm inside you, too?"

My cheeks heated as I nodded.

"All right, step back."

"I'm immortal now, love, you can't kill me."

I smiled. He was. I didn't have to worry about losing him.

I opened my mouth and sang the highest-pitched note I could make. Around us, ice fractured and then broke. Wave after wave of the note echoed into the air. The icy ground under my feet broke. Mother and Father staggered free from their icy prison. Mother stepped to my side and joined me in song. Every person in the garden broke free and fell to their knees. The ice vanished beneath our feet. We kept singing though, sending the note out into the rest of the realm, breaking the icy tomb I'd placed on everything in my despair at losing Brandon. But I didn't lose him. The hope and love for him came through the note and soon the Earth was free from my powers. Mother stopped singing, and so did I. She hugged me.

"I'm so proud of you."

I shuddered in her embrace. "Proud of me fixing what I made?"

"I'm always proud of you and your brothers and sisters, no matter what you do."

We parted and turned to look at Father talking to Brandon a short distance away.

"What do you think they're talking about?"

"I'm sure your father is being kind," Mother said. "We saw everything that happened."

"You did?"

"Aye."

"Will you tell Lorcan and Pepper?"

"I'll leave that honor to you. It was Dia who told you, after all."

"We've had enough surprises in the family now."

Mother laughed. "We certainly have. I'm ready for the peace and happiness Dia promised."

"Me too."

Brandon's mother interrupted his talk with Father and embraced him. She sobbed, touched his crown, and sobbed some more. I walked over to them to offer him support in any way he needed me.

"I'm still me, ma," Brandon said. "Think of it this way. At least I'm immortal now."

She dashed away her tears and hugged him again. "I'm glad if I never have to see you dying before my eyes again."

They parted and Alister hugged him next. His grandfather pursed his lips and then nodded his head as though he'd expected Brandon to become something great.

"This changes everything," Alister said. "If God made you Fae... then..."

"I'll still help the Fellowship. I trained for years, and I won't give that up because I am Fae now." Brandon clasped Alister's shoulder. "This will bring us even closer together."

Alister nodded. "The two will become one again."

"We still need to fix Earth for that to happen fully," I said. "I made a promise."

"It will take a combined effort from all of us," Father said.

"I was thinking when I was singing how much easier it would be if there were multiple places on Earth having the same power thrust into it. If all of us take a different place on Earth and use our power to meet in the center, then they should all combine to fix everything at once. It's like I can see it in a painting, all our colors and powers swirling and mixing and making it beautiful once more."

Mother clasped my hand. "Let's arrange it with your brothers and sisters."

After convincing Brandon's mother we would return, we left for the Summer Court where we'd left my brothers and sisters. Everyone had once again converged in the grand dining hall except there was no food. They all stared at me and Brandon as though we were an illusion after I'd explained everything that had happened and all the secrets that were no longer secret.

"So, Dia, the Dia, made Brandon a Fae?" Aislinn asked.

"Aye," I said.

"And Pepper is a descendant of Dia?" Lorcan asked.

"Aye."

Lorcan looked at Pepper, whose face was pale white.

"Pepper, that's pretty hot." He slid a hand around her shoulder and kissed her open mouth.

"And Mother is a descendant of the Siren Queen and a Rage Demon?" Briana asked.

"Aye."

She rocked back in her chair.

"I think it's awesome we all have this extended family now," Sledge said.

"What does that make Ailbhe, then?" Saoirse asked.

"Special," Arrow said.

Everyone murmured their agreement.

I met Rian's gaze over the table. "What's your question?"

"Have you two marked each other?"

"Well, that's personal." I folded my arms.

"Personal or not, we appear stronger when we're with our fated and marked mate."

"I accidentally marked him, but we haven't had a chance for him to mark me. We don't have time for me to be in the Quiet."

"He doesn't have many years of memories for you to experience, Roisin," Rian said. "You won't be in the Quiet for long."

Sophia slid her hand on top of Rian's, silencing him.

"He's right," Ciara said. "You need to let Brandon mark you before we fix Earth."

"But I promised Dia."

"Did he give you a time limit?"

"No, but..."

"But Malachi and I believe your plan will work but not unless we're all united and at our strongest," Ciara said. "I suggest everyone return to their rooms and get some sleep tonight and tomorrow, if Roisin is awake from the Quiet, then we'll all go to Earth and fix it."

"Agreed," Father said. "It's a lot to absorb and we all need a moment with our mate to take it all in."

"We both love you all so much," Mother said. "We'll meet back here for breakfast."

Everyone stood and left. Brandon sat by my side, waiting for me to make the move.

"Roisin." He brushed my hair from my shoulder and kissed my neck now we were alone. "What's wrong? Don't you want me to mark you?"

"I do. Never consider I don't want you." I turned in my seat.

"Then talk to me."

"What if Dia decides I took too long to fulfill my promise, and he takes you away from me?"

He cupped my face in his warm, firm hands that had suddenly glowed with his new power, sending a delicate sky-blue glow over his palms.

"He won't take me away from you. I promise."

"How can you know that for sure?"

"Did you look around the table tonight?"

I frowned. I'd seen my family.

"Did you see how glad everyone was to be with their fated mate? The strength they took from each other and returned it tenfold? No God would take that away. Not the one I believe in."

I placed my palms over his hands and let my power flare a small fraction into his. The pure white of my power merged with his blue, making it appear as though a cloudy summer sky hovered between us.

"That tickles," he said.

"Are you ready to learn everything about me?"

"Am I ever." He kissed me sweetly on the lips, then urged me to stand. "More than ever am I ready to be inside you again."

I laughed and took his hand in mine and led him through the grand marble hallways of the palace.

"How big is this place?"

"Big enough."

"It's bigger than the demon castle, but I wouldn't mention that to them. They'd take offense."

I laughed, then paused outside my bed chambers.

"It's a little messy inside."

"I only care about you."

I opened the door and pulled him inside with me, cringing at the mess I'd left of half-finished sketches, poems, and paintings on every available surface. Finished works of art hung from the walls.

Brandon walked around the room, studying each piece of art one at a time. Finally, he turned to me and said, "You are talented."

Heat worked its way to my cheeks.

"I love it when you blush." He stepped closer. "So how do I mark you?"

"Your power should do it for you instinctively."

I lifted his hand and placed it on my chest. "Here. This is the place you'll put it."

His hands flared with power, and he yanked them away. "Damn, that was strong."

"Our powers are strong."

"Let's get you naked," he said, bending and gathering the hem of my dress.

I lifted my hands over my head and let him undress me.

"You take my breath away every time I look at you."

My skin pulsed with the need for him to touch me. To put his mating mark on my chest and make me his. Slowly, he lifted his hands to his clothes and undressed.

"This feels like our first time again." He let out a husky chuckle.

I stroked my hands down the muscular expanse of his chest, then wrapped a hand around his cock. His hips jerked forward into my palm.

"You feel so good," he whispered, bringing his mouth to my neck and backing me toward the wall.

My back hit the wall and his body kept coming until he squashed my hand between us, and I couldn't move it like I had been.

"I'm coming in you while I mark you," he said. "And you'll be coming too."

"Is that a promise or a threat?" I smiled.

"Promise all the way."

I lifted a leg and hooked it around his hip, trying to line his cock up with my slick core.

"In a hurry for me?" He cocked an eyebrow.

"I'm so ravenous without you." I rolled my hips the tiny fraction I could with him pinning me to the wall.

"Same, love, same."

He lowered his head and kissed me. Our lips joined as though we'd kissed for a thousand years. Dancing and molding to the other. Frustration bubbled up that he was so close to where I wanted him most. He trailed his lips down my neck and then lowered to the swell of my breast. His mouth closed over the firm peak of my nipple, and I cried out from the instant connection to my core.

"Lift your other leg and let go of my cock."

I did as he said. The new position put him straight at my entrance and I wanted to sing with happiness, but his mouth moved to my other nipple, sucking the peak until it was hard and wet. Then he switched back to the other nipple.

"Brandon," I begged desperate to have him fill the ache inside me.

"You want me?"

"Aye. Now."

He shifted a fraction, so his cock slid inside me. I shuddered knowing this was what I needed, what we both needed. His hips thrust into mine, hitting many pleasure spots. My hands clasped his muscular shoulders, but his firm hands kept me up with ease. Each suction on my nipple joined with the friction of his cock rubbing along my inner walls. My legs shook around his waist, but I refused to let go. One of his hands lifted to my chest and warmth filled my heart. My entire body.

The tension released from my body, and I came on his still-thrusting cock. My chest seared with the pain of his mating mark. I'd deliberately kept that part from him. He didn't need to grasp he was hurting me. He wouldn't have suffered the pain of my mark when I'd marked him while he was so close to death. My vision wavered as images of Brandon as a young child filtered into my mind.

"Hurry," I said sensing I only had a second left before the Quiet claimed me.

Brandon came with a shudder, sending another wave of pleasure inside me at the pulsing of his cock. His mouth lifted from my nipple and the last thing I remembered was his lips brushing my forehead in a tender kiss as I gave myself over to his memories and fell into the Quiet.

CHAPTER THIRTY-THREE
BRANDON

ROISIN UNCONSCIOUS DID STRANGE things to me. I carried her into the bathroom and cleaned her, dried her, then placed her in the bed and settled the covers over her. I returned to the bathroom and washed, then, draped in a towel, I walked around her room, and the adjoining sitting room I hadn't noticed earlier.

Her sketches and paintings were works of art to rival art galleries. Maybe I'd get her work in one or two, or hell even every single one. She deserved it after fighting for me to be hers. I was the luckiest man alive, or should I say Fae?

A knock sounded on the door, and I crossed the room to open it. Rian and Lorcan stood on the other side of the door.

"Shite, the clothes haven't come yet," Lorcan said.

"What clothes?"

"Mother requested the seamstresses make your clothes fitting of Fae royalty," Rian said. "Did you convince Roisin to let you mark her?"

"I did." I opened the door enough, so they saw her asleep on the bed, although it looked like a deeper sleep than just sleeping.

"Good. Let's go."

"Where?"

"Father wants us to test your powers."

"What can I do?"

"That's what we want to find out." Rian turned. "Ah, here comes the seamstress now."

A woman rushed forward and offered me an armful of clothes.

"Thanks," I said, taking them.

"Hurry," Lorcan said. "Roisin won't be out long."

I glanced at Roisin. "How can you be sure?"

"Her breathing isn't deep already." Rian pointed at her form.

"We should wait for her."

"No, she'll want to go straight to Earth."

"True," I said. "Give me a minute to dress."

I shut the door feeling guilty about leaving Roisin and sneaking off with her brothers, but this was her home, so I had every faith that if she woke before I came back, she'd find me. As she'd told me, the mating mark meant she'd find me anywhere I went now. I dressed quickly, glad I'd be able to find her too.

Lorcan and Rian were lounging against the wall when I opened the door.

"Aren't you meant to be spending time with your mates?" I asked.

"We have, and we'll be back with them soon. This won't take long," Lorcan said.

They hurried through the marble hallways, taking turn after turn and making me lose all sense of direction. At least I'd marked Roisin, and I'd be able to find my way back to her room by that. Even now, I sensed the pull between us. We walked through a set of large columns and into a wide courtyard.

"This is where we train," Lorcan said with a wicked grin. He spun around and flung a jolt of power at me.

It hit me square in the chest and knocked me off my feet.

"You're supposed to use your power to block."

I held up my glowing hands. They shone a sky-blue. "What is my power?"

Rian and Lorcan whispered to each other as I got to my feet.

Lorcan flung another wave of power at me, but I ducked to the left in time to avoid it.

"Use your power," Rian said.

I shook my hands, but they only glowed. "I trained with swords and fists, not magical powers."

"Same thing," Rian said.

"No, it's not." I ducked to avoid another flare of Lorcan's power. "Swords are tangible. This power I can't hold."

"You don't need to hold it. Control it," Rian said.

Lorcan sent more flares of power like small glowing orbs of flames my way one after another not giving me a chance to dodge them. One took my feet out from under me, and I landed on my back with a loud harrumph coming from my chest.

"I don't get it." I lifted my hands to the sky in frustration. Power shot up, and a flare of sky-blue magic shot into the sky, merging with it and disappearing instantly. Then a swarm of birds flew into the courtyard. They circled above me as though waiting for my direction. I rolled to the side and pointed at Lorcan.

They flew toward him, then at the last second, Lorcan's power shot out and changed, directing the birds back into the sky.

"Animals," Lorcan said.

"Makes sense that would be Roisin's fated mate's power since she's always loved the unicorns but could never get close to them," Rian said.

I scrambled to my feet. "You mean I can control animals?"

"Aye," Rian said. "We'd wondered if you'd have access to all the elemental powers, but it doesn't look like it."

"How do I control them?"

Rian rolled his eyes. "With your powers."

"But how? All I did was throw my hands into the air with frustration."

Lorcan laughed. "Don't worry, you'll get the hang of it."

Roisin walked into the courtyard. "He'll get the hang of what?"

"His powers over animals," Lorcan said.

Roisin folded her arms over her chest. "You took my mate for power training without asking me?"

"Relax, he was fine," Lorcan said.

Roisin flicked her gaze over me. If I'd been human, some of those hits he'd flung at me would have left bruises, but now I was Fae, I suffered nothing.

I grinned and strode over to her. "He's right. I was fine. Better than fine. I now understand more about what I've become."

"I would have helped you figure it out." Roisin pouted.

"We'll see you both in the morning," Rian said. "I'm heading back to bed with Sophia."

"Me too," Lorcan said, then laughed. "I meant with Pepper."

Her brothers shoved each other as they left the courtyard.

"So, you've trained your powers here?" I ran my gaze over Roisin, getting hard for her all over again.

"Aye." She kept her annoyed stance.

"You woke quickly. Wasn't much to see?"

She dropped her arms. "There was plenty to see. Especially a lot of women."

"Shit. Sorry. I didn't realize you'd see those memories."

"I saw all of them, Brandon." She huffed. "I understand you have a past."

I walked toward her slowly. "So, you comprehend none of them didn't matter until I found you."

Her expression eased.

"If I could go back and change it and wait for you, then I would."

"I believe you."

"So, we're good?"

"Aye."

"Can I take you back to bed?"

Her cheeks flushed a delicate pink.

"Perhaps." She twirled a strand of hair around her finger.

"I promise to make it up to you and wipe all those images from your mind with hours upon hours of orgasms."

"Well," she said. "You promised me that and you still haven't delivered."

I laughed and grabbed her hand, urging her to follow me from the courtyard.

"Do you even comprehend where you're going?" she asked, still laughing at my eagerness to have her alone and naked again.

"Nope." I laughed.

She tugged my hand to the left.

"Lead the way, Princess. I'll always follow you."

CHAPTER THIRTY-FOUR

ROISIN

BRANDON FINALLY MADE GOOD on his hours-long loving session. My body was limp from all the orgasms he'd given me. A blush heated my cheeks as we met my family for breakfast. I still blushed when Brandon and I walked from the Veil back into the enclosed garden of the Fellowship.

I was probably still blushing now as we stood waiting for the cue to heal the Earth.

Pepper had made us small stones each that would glow at the same time, so we would all comprehend when to feed our powers into the Earth.

Brandon's mother hovered nervously near us, as did his grandfather and the rest of the Fellowship.

We ended up picking the power points. Places we recognized were great power.

Saoirse and Briana were in Crystal Creek with their mates standing by for support at the waterfall where Saoirse had given birth.

Me and Aislinn were here in Ireland in the spring with Brandon and Fallon as our support.

Rian and Ciara with Sophia and Malachi were at the Amazon River near the jaguar shifter colony.

Lorcan and Father with Pepper and Mother were at the old Water Sprite Everglades where Lorcan had killed the last living Trapper.

Four points where powerful magic lived to help us in our quest to save Earth.

Nervous energy zinged through my hands. It was as though my power comprehended it was about to do something great. Something so magical it hungered for it.

"Do you sense it building?" I whispered to Aislinn.

"Aye," she said, twirling a dagger around her fingers.

The stone glowed a bright green like a cat's eye.

Aislinn nodded at me and sheathed the dagger. We kneeled and placed our hands on the ground. Our power flared, lighting our hands. I pushed it forward into the soil. Into the very essence of the Earth. On and on I sent my power forward, but it wasn't working like I thought it would.

"Brandon?"

"What do you need?"

"You. I need you."

He kneeled in front of me and placed his hands on top of mine. His hands flared bright with his power and sent that extra bit of magic the Earth needed.

Fallon copied Brandon and placed his palms over Aislinn's hands. She lifted her head and smiled at him.

"It's working."

"It is!"

The Earth sucked our powers into it like a sponge taking all that we offered and as it healed and mended to its former self, it kept taking.

Taking and taking.

Draining us.

If we didn't break the connection, the Earth would drain us dry. Punish us for leaving it to suffer without our aid.

I tried yanking my hands away, but they wouldn't move.

"Aislinn, can you stop?" I asked, trying to keep the panic out of my voice but failing.

"No." She scowled.

"What do we do?" I stared into Brandon's face.

I couldn't have him make me his for us to end now. Would draining our powers kill us? Whatever the Earth was doing, it was putting a strain on us. All my muscles were sore. Sweat dripped from my forehead.

"I can't stop either." I stared at the glowing stone. Was my entire family in the same predicament? Had my idea sent us to our demise?

And then a pair of arms were lifting me from the ground. Big arms with taloned fingers broke the connection. I looked up and up into the concerned eyes of the Beast.

"We will not lose our family now we've just found you."

My power stopped flowing to my hands. "My sister."

He placed me on the ground, and I rushed over to Brandon, who was sitting dazedly on the ground, staring at his hands.

The Beast picked my sister off the ground and severed her connection, too. Aislinn looked ready to grab one of her daggers and stab him, so I scrambled to my feet.

"He's family," I said as the Beast lowered her to the ground.

"What about everyone else? We have to stop them."

The Beast smirked. "No need. We've got it covered. Rex is with your father. Tay is with your other siblings, and Thea is with the rest. They're already on their way here."

"Thank you." I hugged the hulking demon.

He patted my back gently. "Time for another party?"

"No," Brandon said, coming to take me into his arms. "The last party the demons had, I almost died."

"Ah but look at you now."

"Besides," Rexan said, appearing through a portal with my parents, Lorcan, and Pepper. "Your father wants to see you again."

"Your father is alive?" Brandon's mother rushed through the crowd that was growing bigger every second.

"He is, but..."

"What?"

"The Winter Court ages humans prematurely," the Demon King said. "He doesn't have many years left."

"Please," Brandon's mother said. "Bring him home."

The Demon King vanished into a portal.

CHAPTER THIRTY-FIVE
BRANDON'

MY FATHER. THE MAN I'd thought had abandoned me and my family arrived by the side of the Demon King. He was right. The old man had little time left in him, but I'd take whatever time we had left. So would my mother.

She rushed into his outstretched arms as though she didn't care he looked older than her father. She'd taken my explanation for his disappearance better than I'd expected.

Love. Unconditional love.

I had that love now with Roisin.

My Fae Princess.

She wrapped her arms around me from behind and rested her chin on my shoulder.

"We'll stay here for now."

"Really?"

"Aye." She kissed the side of my cheek. "We have forever to explore. What's a few more years here?"

"I love you so much." I choked on the emotion clogging my throat.

"Go," she said. "Make peace with your father. I saw how much his absence hurt you. I saw the memory you saw in that forest. How it wasn't his choice to leave you. I hope it heals your wounds."

I lifted her hand and kissed it. She let me go and I walked over to my father. He released the tight hold he had on my mother and stepped toward me on his shaky legs.

"Son, please forgive me. I never meant to hurt you."

"Yes."

His gaze flicked up to my crown.

"You're... you..."

"I'm a Fae now."

"Not possible," he said.

I smiled. "Anything is possible when you have a love so great it changes the entire world as we know it."

I glanced over at Roisin talking to her sister Briana. Roisin looked happy. Content. Her gaze met mine across the garden. Around her, the flowers burst into bloom, the garden reshaped into a once glorious place. Briana smiled too. The sisters hugged.

My new family.

My new future.

I stepped toward my father and hugged him. He was my family, too. Now and forever, the Fae and the humans would live in harmony. All because I'd fallen in love with a Fae Princess and she'd fallen in love with me.

Being fated to her was the icing on the top of this magical ending. Which was the beginning of our happily ever after. To all our happily ever afters.

ROISIN

Sunlight streamed through the trees. Warmth caressed our limbs. The Summer Court was no longer our gilded prison. Fae came and went to Earth as they pleased. Everyone was happy. No one more so than me.

The breeze ruffled my hair as we rode the Unicorn across the fields of the Summer Court. Brandon's power over animals had let us make friends with the allusive creature. Once we'd both learned how to ride the magnificent Unicorns without falling off, we did so every time we returned to the Fae Kingdom.

Brandon's arms wrapped around my waist, holding me in place. Tight against his body. My favorite place to be. His lips kissed the side of my neck.

"I love it here."

"Me too." I tilted my head back and rested it on his chest.

His palms flared with his powers, and the Unicorn surged into a gallop. I laughed as I wrapped my fingers in its silky mane.

"In a hurry to go somewhere?" I asked.

"Always with you. No matter how long we're together, being alone with you is still the best place in all the realms."

I couldn't agree with him more. Being with my fated mate was worth everything we endured. Worth every heartache, pain, and suffering.

Because once you found true love, there was no better place to be except with the one who loved you, accepted you for who you were, and would stand by your side through the good times and the bad.

A love that would last forever.

The End

1. Fae's Song

2. Fae's Wolf

3. Fae's Alpha

4. Fae's Heart

5. Fae's Witch

6. Fae's Dream

7. Fae's Fate

8. Fae's Love

ACKNOWLEDGMENTS

First, thank you to my family for putting up with me disappearing into the world of books. A special thank you to my daughter Sarah for designing my beautiful covers. To Belinda, thank you for encouraging me to write again after I lost everything in a computer crash. Remember to back up! A lot of work goes into creating a story, and I'm always thankful for the support of my online writing buddies, beta readers, and fellow authors, Immy for always making me smile, Tammy for believing in me from the start, Karen for being willing to read any level of heat I write, Cassie for her hand holding, Lana for her invaluable knowledge. The biggest thank you goes to my 'twin' Dannielle, who is the best critique partner, cheerleader, and sounding board ever, and is forever fixing my comma errors, sorry Dannielle I'm afraid you're stuck with them and me. Finally thank you to all you romance readers. You are my tribe.

ALSO BY

FANTASY AND PARANORMAL ROMANCE
Summer Court

Fae's Song

Fae's Wolf

Fae's Alpha

Fae's Heart

Fae's Witch

Fae's Dream

Fae's Fate

Fae's Love

Anthologies

Reluctant Bride

Alpha Male

HELEN WALTON

ABOUT AUTHOR

Helen Walton is a tea drinking, chocoholic, romance writer. Stories are her obsession. She adores creating sensual romances containing a sprinkling of humor and the all-important happy ending. She lives in South Australia with her family, and menagerie of quirky animals where they all take her away from her book world and demand to be fed. Lucky for them, she enjoys cooking but prefers baking.

Sign up for my newsletter for exclusive content.

https://www.helenwaltonauthor.com/newsletter

Visit my website

https://www.helenwaltonauthor.com/

Follow me

bookbub.com/profile/helen-walton

facebook.com/Helen-Walton-Author-103496667706602/

goodreads.com/author/show/20249188.Helen_Walton

instagram.com/helen.walton.author

tiktok.com/@helen.walton.author